Advance

The March of the Orphans

And The Battle of Stones River

"Good historical fiction should make it a challenge for the reader to discern the difference between actual and imagined events, creating a cohesive narrative that enhances our connection with the past.

The March of the Orphans And the Battle of Stones River does just that for those wanting to take a fresh look at the Battle of Stones River and the famed First Kentucky Brigade.

Horgan has written a compelling account that reminds us of the thousands of human stories playing out while the battle raged on. Readers who prefer a good story and historians alike will enjoy this book."

Jim Lewis, Park Ranger, Stones River Battlefield National Park, Murfreesboro, Tennessee

Praise For ***Kevin Horgan's*** first book:

The March of the 18th, A Story of Crippled Heroes in the Civil War

"Our nation can be held accountable for its regard for the injured who risked all to defend her. This book, and the author's generous mission, is a high standard worthy of our respect."

Jared Ogden, former US Navy SEAL, CEO of *Phoenix Patriot Foundation,* and star of National Geographic Channel's *Ultimate Survivor Alaska*

"Courage, leadership, and loyalty are just a few words that describe the group of characters in this Civil War story."

Don Bonsper, Lt Colonel USMC (ret), Author of Vietnam Memoirs, My Experiences as a Marine Platoon Leader

"Horgan expresses the emotional turmoil, the isolation and the sense of hopelessness of those overwhelmed by physical and emotional disabilities. The March of the 18th is a very well written and insightful work by an author who understands so much more than is expressed in deployed morning reports."

Gerard R. Tuttle, PhD, Colonel USAF (ret), 25 year psychotherapist

"A little known piece of American history that should be taught in our schools. Three cheers for the courage of the Veterans' Reserve Corps, and The March of the 18th!

Zellie Orr, Lecturer and Author of First Top Guns, An Account of the "Last Hurrah" of the segregated 332nd FG (a/k/a Tuskegee Airmen)

"A fast paced historical novel that brings to life a unit of Civil War heroes long forgotten as a foot-note in our nation's history. Read this book; you won't be disappointed!"

Mike Pierce, PhD, Major USA (ret), CEO and Founder of New Horizons For Heroes

"Horgan has honored the memory of the wounded warriors of the Civil War, has educated us on their challenges and their triumphs, and has inspired all of us to do more for the extraordinary heroes among us today."

James S. Sfayer, Lt Colonel USMC (ret), USMA Superintendent's Award for Instructional Excellence, and 2005 Walt Disney Teacher Award Winner

The MARCH of the ORPHANS

And The Battle of Stones River

KEVIN HORGAN

The March of the Orphans
And The Battle of Stones River
by Kevin Horgan

Printed in the United States of America.

ISBN 9781498441858

This is a work of fiction with a historical basis.

Photos and Map are from the National Park Service Archives, with annotations by the author.

www.kevinhorganbooks.com

www.xulonpress.com

Dedicated to the memory of two great Marines
now guarding Heaven's Gates.

Daniel W. Horgan,
My father
and
Harold K. Grune,
My father-in-law

Semper fi, gentlemen.
Well done.

Major General John C.
Breckinridge CSA

General Braxton Bragg, CSA

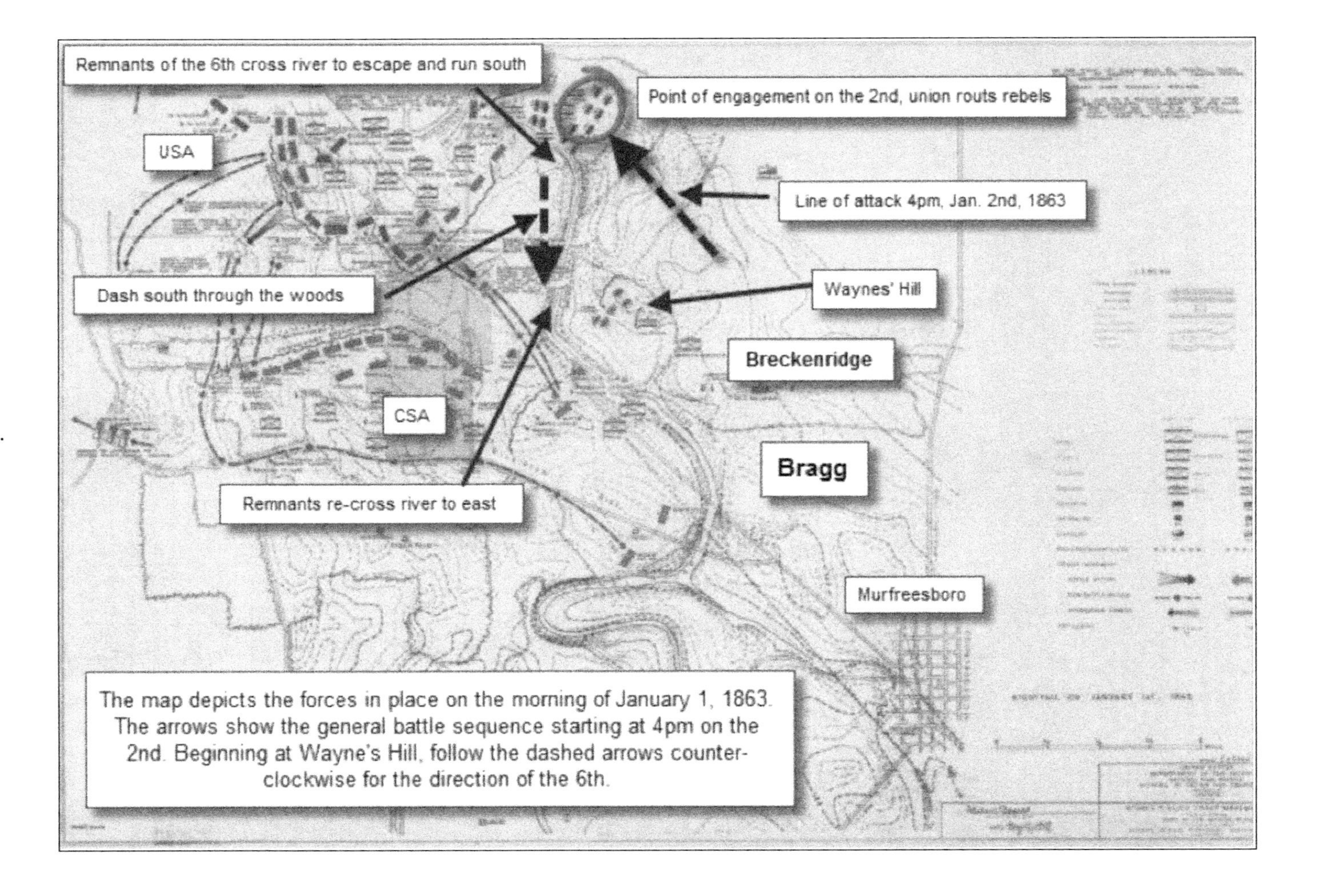
Remnants of the 6th cross river to escape and run south
Point of engagement on the 2nd, union routs rebels
USA
Line of attack 4pm, Jan. 2nd, 1863
Dash south through the woods
Waynes' Hill
Breckenridge
CSA
Bragg
Remnants re-cross river to east
Murfreesboro
The map depicts the forces in place on the morning of January 1, 1863. The arrows show the general battle sequence starting at 4pm on the 2nd. Beginning at Wayne's Hill, follow the dashed arrows counter-clockwise for the direction of the 6th.

Table of Contents

Prologue

Sitting on a bench at the Stones River Battlefield in Murfreesboro, Tennessee, mid-morning, Louis Freedman watched the flight of a hawk high above in the trees, whose leaves sparkled in gray, green and white in the light breeze. Even in November the cool air and warm sun invited everyone and anyone to enjoy the day, doing nothing but listening, watching, and dreaming about the history surrounding the grounds. Louis embraced the solitude, and lost sight of the graceful bird as it floated away.

A large black short haired dog was sniffing at Louis' outstretched hand, and he curled his fingers gently, tickled by the cold snout and rapid tentative licks from the mutt.

"She likes you."

"She's a he, I think."

"Oh, I don't know, but Pumpkin doesn't like men, so *this,*" and the girl nodded toward the dog, "is *huge*." The girl was in her mid-twenties, lots of hair messily stuffed under a hoodie, with big expressive eyes with something odd about them; he couldn't tell quite what it was. She had a brilliant smile and was small in height but with the kind of curves Louis appreciated. About his age. He smiled in return.

"Now why doesn't Pumpkin like men?"

"Rescue dog. I've had her a month, and she or he or whatever is *terrified,*" the exaggeration of her words was her signature, "of guys. But not *you*!"

"I'm a likeable guy, I think." His smile faded.

A family van parked in the near empty side lot a few feet away. Parents and kids tumbled out, shouting and yelling, which spooked Pumpkin, who stopped sniffing. One kid started throwing a ball high in the air above his head, and failed catching it on the way down. The large expanse of the park became much smaller around the one bench. The kid heaved the ball skyward again.

The uncaught ball rolled and stopped between Louis' feet. He tensed, and stared at it. Pumpkin recoiled silently, as if sensing it was about to be stricken.

"You okay, mister?" The kid, two feet away, expected Louis to hand him the ball.

Louis continued to stare at it, unmoving. The roar in his ears froze him completely. To him, it wasn't just a kid's ball.

The girl reached for it, stood, and heaved it nearly half a football field away. "Good luck, you little creep." To the family she barked, "This park is so *huge*, and you have to crowd us, *here*? There's a *thousand* places to park and a million *things* to see, and you practically wanna *kick us off* this bench? *Huh*?"

The girl had assumed a faux-fighting stance, arms spread, shoulders dropped, and her head bobbed in anticipation.

The parents stared back, and it appeared that the hapless dad was going to chastise Louis and the girl. Pumpkin growled. The clueless mom sang a cheery "Let's go over here!" With that the family was on its way.

"Nice. Subtle." Louis started breathing again.

"Thanks! It's not a good day unless I can pick a fight," she said, shaking her head in bewilderment.

"So, Rambo-lady, what's your name?" Pumpkin had gone back to licking Louis' hand.

"Shannon." Her smile was infectious, and she unzipped her sweatshirt half way, and pushed the hood off her head. Light brown blondish hair, lots of it. She shook it out, and Louis gave her an appreciative grin in return.

"Hi, Shannon. I'm Louis." He stood, and extended his hand. She gripped it and wouldn't let it go.

"The ball," she said.

"Oh. That." He thought her grip, firm but very soft, was awkward, but it had been a long time, too long, since he had simply held a pretty girl's hand.

Pumpkin whined. Shannon arched an eyebrow, and she coaxed Louis to sit, still holding his hand. She sat close to him, now holding his hand in both of hers. Big eyes from her, and Louis wanted to explain, but couldn't.

"It's nothing."

"I can see the tats, Louis. My brother served. Army?"

"No. Marines. With 3/5 in Afghanistan until a year ago."

"*Ooorah*, man! We're a Marine *family*!" She launched into her own family history, father, uncles, grandfather, brother, cousins. Louis heard little of it.

He smiled, then frowned. Shannon kept her eyes glued to him.

"Hey, uh, Pumpkin likes you. She knows you're hurting. Dogs *know*, ya know? And you're not *too* funny looking and well…" The mega-watt smile.

"I was gonna ask you to run away with me, but I didn't want you to break my fingers." He returned her smile. Shannon was friendly, pretty, and smelled good. He couldn't resist the flirtation.

"I have a confession, Shannon. Just for you. I'm ready to tell it. The truth."

Shannon gripped his hand hard, and inched closer, and with a sharp intake of breath braced herself to hear the trials of this young Marine veteran.

"I had two sausage McMuffins about half an hour ago. I think Pumpkin likes them as much as I do."

Shannon gasped, laughed, shook her head and stood, hands on hips. Pumpkin kept at Louis' hand, content.

"*Okay,* hero. I have *your* number! You're a *knucklehead,*" with a wonderful laugh.

Her smile would light the bottom of the ocean, he thought, but calling him a hero cut to that place in his chest that never stopped aching.

"Look, Shannon, I'm no hero."

"Yeah, but..."

"No, please. I'm not. I survived. The guys I served with who didn't come back, well, they're the heroes. My best buddy has a TBI and he'll never be the same, not even close." Louis paused, eyes misty, realized he was too intense too quickly, and put his hands on his head. He forced a smile. "He's a hero. I survived, but I'm not sure what I am, or where I'm going."

Shannon put out her hand, palm up, and wiggled her fingers at him. "Let's walk, okay? Then I can see if Pumpkin *really* likes you."

Louis stood, awkwardly unstable, and he tried to laugh it off.

"Yeah, good idea, let's walk." He could feel his good-self returning quickly in the company of this sweet young woman. "So, Shannon, why is a big black lab called Pumpkin?"

"*Listen,* tough guy, I'll call her *anything* I want!"

"Him, you mean."

"Whatever. Say, there's a monument a half mile from here I like to go to. It's the first permanent one of the *entire* Civil War! That's *so* important, you know?"

As they began their walk, side by side with Pumpkin staying close to Shannon, Louis thought that, yes, a monument to the Civil War commemorating the Battle of Stones River, and the sacrifice of both North and South, was certainly more than important.

A monument honoring the dead was then, and would always be, a moral necessity.

@@@

Part One
Orphans

I will not leave you as orphans...
John 14:18

1
Summer 1862

The prisoner woke smelling the stink of wet fur, acutely pungent amid the stench of vomit, sweat, and waste. He tried to open one eye as the hammering pain in his head continued its incessant beat. He was hungry, thirsty beyond compare, and the wet hair was different and very close to his nose, which had made his stomach growl. He opened the one eye, just a sliver, and then shot both lids open, frozen.

Two rats were gnawing at something unfamiliar not an inch from his face. They were large, and he thought absurdly that both could fit inside his head if they had wanted to go there. The rats had started chewing and nibbling on the object, testing both it and the resolve of the other vermin to obtain it. They became more aggressive over the thing, which looked like a piece of bone. Each grasped and bit, chewed and gnawed, neither getting real purchase. Then the gray streaked rat bit the deep brown rodent on the snout.

The prisoner moved his head back as the gray rat whipped its tail across the bridge of the man's nose. The tail cut him, and he could taste the blood and now was fully awake. The rats stopped fighting over the bone. The brown one scurried away from the prisoner as the gray one sniffed and lapped at the fresh blood on the floor.

The prisoner, now on his knees, in a blind fury slammed his right fist down, catching the gray rat square in the back, and the animal squealed and pulsed and ran away crookedly. The brown rat had already scurried a few feet away, but kept its little eyes riveted on the prisoner.

"I don't like you, either."

Keys clanged as a large metal door swung outward, the sound sending punches of pain through the front of the prisoner's head.

"Let's go, soldier. No more beauty rest for you. You're going back to your unit now." The jailor was ancient, stooped, and hacked a phlegmy cough between sentences.

"Why don't you blow that snot out?"

"What? Never! Keeps me healthy. Fights off the bad air!" The jailor spoke this as if an absolute truth known for all time, and sucked up more snot and hacked it out in another wet cough.

"I have to relieve myself. Leave the door open."

"No. Use the bucket. Make it quick." The door clanged shut amidst coughing.

The prisoner knew there was no bucket, but he did his business just the same, using one of his socks to clean himself.

"Rats, no paper, no bucket. Don't think I'm coming back here," he said to no one, banging on the door twice. He felt the rising sting of a welt across his cheek and nose, the small trail of blood now dried. "I have to stop drinking, too."

The door opened again with a familiar clang, and a tall lanky soldier, unkempt and just the worse for wear as the prisoner, grinned lewdly, showing the backs of his hands. They were bloody and swollen.

"James Time, I hope you had as much fun as I did," said the grinning Rebel, about ten years younger than Time's forty. "A heckuva night. Wish you were there!" He dropped his hands but kept the smile. Garadon had an arresting feature that kept most men at a distance. One of his eyes was bright green, and the other a pale blue. His grin forced a perpetual squint, but his eyes were alarming when he looked directly at a stranger, and Garadon knew it gave off a certain aura of insanity.

"You weren't beating on walls, were you, Garadon?"

"No, my friend, just another poor couple of drunks wanting to steal my coat. They won't be needing one for a while, my guess." Garadon shook his hands out as if drying them, wincing as he did so.

The jailor coughed and called out, "A bushwhacker is here for the lot of you!"

Time and Garadon made their way to an open wagon with three other Rebel soldiers, all of them having spent two days and a night without food and water in the hell-hole of Charleston's notorious prison. As Rebel soldiers, guilty of no more than an errant night with a hazy memory, their rotting in the jail for two days was punishment enough. The five dehydrated and exhausted soldiers climbed aboard the open wagon, with a provost, an appointed military policeman, holding the reins of a single mule. He was a true provost, not a bushwhacker as told by the jailor, and the distinction was crucial. The provost was a military man, with a mission and the authority of a legitimate military appointment. A bushwhacker was good for little except causing hate and discontent, and occasionally finding and holding accountable deserters or Union supporters, as long as there was profit. Jail was better treatment than at their hands, for the most part.

Garadon asked the provost, accompanied with a smile, "You have some water? Nothing for us since we got here."

"You'd think we were Yankees," said the northerner by birth, now Confederate soldier, James Time.

"Here, help yourself. You boys all right?" The provost showed genuine concern for the others, three young soldiers who possessed a hollow, unbroken stare but drank the water with abandon using the ladles provided.

Garadon arched an eye at Time. "You think you're funny. I spent the last two days with Yankee prisoners. They had a difficult time of it." He displayed his knuckles again, and blew air on them.

Time was unimpressed. "At least you could move around. I was in a metal closet, sleeping in my own filth and nearly eaten by rats. I had almost given up, except I heard your shouts." Time paused and drank two handfuls deeply. "Sounded like you were having yourself a good time."

Garadon drank as Time spoke, seemingly uninterested but taking in every word just as earnestly. "Rats, huh? I'd have eaten one in another hour."

The provost called the men to take seats in the back of the wagon. "And there's salt pork and some hardtack. Not much. Easy now."

Garadon jumped on the buckboard up front with a renewed energy. "I'll ride up front with you, my friend."

The provost smiled, eyeing Garadon's bloodied and swollen hands. "We'll be at camp in time for noon dinner."

Time reached for a small piece of salt pork. He touched a fatty sliver, and realized only then that the object the rats were fighting over back in the jail was the partial bone of a man's finger.

He fell in and out of slumber. The ride was slow and rhythmic, the sounds of Garadon and the driver provost talking animatedly about the war and the antics of soldiers on leave. The other three soldiers were young, barely out of their teens, and they remained with their knees drawn up, heads bowed, and arms hugging their legs. If they slept or not there was no indication, but the silence and resignation to their fate was simple and accepted.

They had a bad night or two, and did not prefer the sunshine or the growing humidity. Going back to camp was not an inducement for celebration. They were afraid.

Time slowly kicked his feet out, nudging one of the soldiers to move a little. The youth, startled, made fists, took one look at Time's blank stare and went back to his reverie without complaint. He moved to accommodate the older man, a corporal by his stripes, with room to spare.

Time liked the sun. He let it bathe the open and uncovered part of his face. His thick brown beard was kept trimmer than the standards of the army, making his face jowly even though he was lean and hard muscled. His crown was bald, and he kept a wide-brimmed non-regulation hat perched toward the back of his head to enjoy the warm sun after two days of cold wet darkness.

The sun ducked behind a fluffy cloud, and he wondered if the cloud was stationary and the sun was hiding from him. He looked directly at the billowing mass and marveled at the contrast of white, gray, black, and the peripheral shock of light blue on a glorious day. The cloud was changing shape, and he spied a turtle in the sky, and almost spoke to a brother he had not seen in over fifteen years. No, he thought, closer to twenty.

"It's a turtle."

"What?" Asked Garadon, who had finally stopped talking.

"Nothing. Enjoying the day." Time smiled, thinking of watching clouds with his younger brother as children in New Jersey many years before. Wonderful days, he mused. Wish I had known that, then. Perfectly wonderful.

He remained in that sleepless world between consciousness and nothingness, remembering with embarrassed clarity his journey since a teenager. An argument with his parents and his failed apprenticeship at gunsmithing, after begging for the opportunity and having dropped academics altogether, was the catalyst for leaving home. The work was a ruse to get out of school, but his real goal was independence with ample opportunity for sloth and trouble. Signing on with sea merchants, rough-necking and drinking too much, enjoying the life of a hard laborer without real responsibility. Time's skills were many, but mostly unborn and unrealized. He was a fine rifle shot, not remarkable, but respected. He had fast hands, and was unafraid to get close to an adversary, so close the risk of being struck was high, and he was as foul an enemy as any man would acknowledge. He sometimes threw the first punch, whether he was armed or not, and invariably threw the last. Time had only taken one beating in his life, and that was in his late teens. He was wary by nature, angry inside, and generally of so sour a disposition that his mere glance was enough for the most bold to take another path.

There was constant back breaking labor over the years from New York to Boston to the Caribbean to Mexico and back, several times a circuit, more than he could count, with occasional land jobs to escape other undesirable perceived hardships. His skin was a conflicted cracked brown and pale white and underneath it all hard as stone. He joined the army twice as a volunteer and been mustered out when not required any longer. He found himself in Charleston in April of 1861, having jumped ship amid rumors of a war. Time had been a denizen of the shadows, a silent dark figure who took little pleasure in anything but his own idle thoughts, a recluse to himself, an orphan of his past, a human in name only, selfish, stern, and fiercely independent. Food, sunlight, sleep and liquor. Occasionally female companionship, though he loved a woman once but she loved another. His brother's wife-to-be. She was his friend, she said, the sweetest girl he ever saw. But she was Jon's prize, not his. Go away, he reflected, as he did every day.

Time thought back to the excitement of Charleston in April of '61. Amid all the rumors the last thing he thought would happen was the firing on Fort Sumter. He chuckled to himself. People believed he had high minded, altruistic reasons for joining the confederacy right away, but the simple truth was that he was losing his sea legs, as he had before, and needed dry land. The prospect of killing men for pay had a certain intangible and cryptic allure.

That was just over a year ago. He opened his eyes as the wagon hit a hole, waking all the passengers, and apparently the provost driver. Time smiled. He hadn't killed anyone on this enlistment, yet, and slipped back into the old habits of food, sunlight, sleep, liquor, and work to pay for it. Rumors had swirled a week ago of moving some of the motley brigade north, but it was the same rumor every week. Food, sunlight, sleep, liquor, work.

"Sorry about that, boys. We're closer, but it'll be rockier here on out."

"Where're our weapons?" Garadon's happy nature on being released from jail had worn off. He was about to mention that he did not recognize the route they were taking, but kept to himself.

"Your sergeant collected 'em," the provost sneered, "And you get 'em when you get back."

Garadon groaned. Time pushed his hat forward to shade his eyes. They did not have a sergeant. Time and Garadon, both corporals, did everything a sergeant would do.

Three horsemen, not in any uniform, emerged from dense scrub and came toward the wagon, moving in the direction of Charleston. The road was narrow and a confrontation was unavoidable. They had the swagger and aloofness of soldiers, but were too old to be effective cavalry. Their age was an immunity, which they handled with a bare minimum of grace.

The leader, soft and saddle weary, his undersized horse overworked, had a face like a squirrel with two bad front teeth. He called out, "Watcha got there?"

The provost brought the wagon to a halt, although he did not need to do so. "Get outa my way. I'm the provost returning these men to the camp up north here. No mind to you, mister."

The buck-toothed rider took umbrage. "I have the authority to ask..."

"The hell you do. These are soldiers of the confederacy. And I have identified myself, so now, git." With practiced hands the provost had a pistol in each hand, arms extended, one pointed at the squirrel-leader's chest, the other in the general direction of the other two horsemen.

But he let go of the reins. One of the riders spooked the mule enough for the wagon to lurch.

In an instant Garadon saw what this was: a robbery, and perhaps murder. The provost lost his balance, arching backwards. The squirrel faced man raised his short rifle and fired as he moved it up, hitting the provost square in the chest and one of the passengers in the head with the buckshot from the large caliber weapon. The provost was dead before he could drop his pistols. The superficially struck soldier screamed.

Garadon grabbed one pistol smoothly and dove across the dead provost, firing in mid-air and striking the squirrel leader in the neck, and then pounced on top of the bleeding bandit. One rider, a fat, sweaty man, kept saying "whoa, whoa," never reaching for a weapon. The third rider turned his long rifle to Garadon, whose back was exposed as he struggled to wrestle the dying leader to the ground. The armed rider couldn't get off a good shot but his intent was lethal. The horses all stepped anxiously as if trying to free themselves from muck.

Time reached over the bleeding soldier, and fished the second pistol from the front floorboard of the wagon, never taking his eyes off the armed bandit, who was trying too hard to get a shot off at Garadon. This rider saw Time in his periphery and chose to dispatch Garadon, now on the ground, first.

A mistake. Garadon turned the now inert but still bleeding carcass of the squirrel leader toward the direction of the rifle barrel, which absorbed the shot but pushed Garadon flat on his back, shaken but unhurt.

Time shot the bandit twice in the center of his chest. The horse reared, and ran with the near-dead rider hanging from one stirrup.

The fat sweaty rider kept saying "whoa" again and again, his hands clenched on the reins of his horse.

"What'll it be, fat man?"

"I, I, I, whoa, now!" The fat bandit was in shock, unable to process what had happened so quickly, and he could not control his horse, shouting at the beast instead of trying to soothe it. The two uninjured soldiers in the wagon jumped out and one ran after the horse that grazed nearby, the dead rider still with one foot screwed into the stirrup. The other soldier walked up to the fat bandit.

"Git off'n my horse."

@@@

The Confederate captain was too pretty to be taken seriously, but his first sergeant was a thick-necked brute whose arms bulged his uniform coat sleeves, taxing the limits of the material and intimidating nearly everyone who entered the captain's tent.

Except Time and Garadon. Neither was easily impressed or rarely intimidated.

The captain had a perfumed silk handkerchief pinched between the thumb and forefinger of his left hand, and continuously dabbed at his nose in a feeble attempt to combat the stench of the camp. In his right hand he held a large feather quill, waving it about in a flamboyant gesture of perceived authority.

The captain sat, his sergeant behind him to his left, as if to avoid the feather quill pen. The sergeant's presence made the tent interior shrink. Time and Garadon stood at a casual parade rest, their rifles now back in their possession.

"What made you," the dandy captain dabbed his nose, "think that this marauder was the provost?"

"As I said, captain, we were in jail for two days and if Abe Lincoln walked in to free us we'd have gone with him." Time's exasperation was painfully evident, bordering on insubordination.

"You should not be insolent, Corporal, uh, Time, is it?" spat the captain, his voice rising, as he looked at his own sergeant, who grunted a non-committal, "Yessir."

Time acted quickly, more deferentially. "Beg your pardon, sir. No water, no food, two days..."

"Of your," a sniff at the kerchief, "own doing, hmmm?"

"Yes, yes, of course, sir. The jailor had no problem releasing us to the impostor. I didn't think..."

"You have demonstrated," again, a sniff, longer and more pronounced, "your lack of thinking!"

"Sir, may I speak?" Garadon's boldness in a fight was part of his nature, as was his willingness to speak his mind.

"Of course, Corporal Garadon, of course." The captain almost brightened when Garadon addressed him, and he obliged the officer with a full-toothed smile.

"Sir, the whole episode was a set-up. Yes, we drank too much and were a little disorderly..."

"A little?" The massive sergeant knew well the men before him.

"Perhaps," another big smile, "perhaps acutely so. But there's more to this. I was way-laid by two bums in my jail cell. They paid dearly for trying to get rough with me, I assure you!" He showed his cut and swollen hands. "And Time here was left for dead. Rat bites!"

The captain cringed, enthralled and wide-eyed. Garadon plunged ahead.

"I was sleeping while riding, that mule moving slow and steady, and before I realized it those three bush-whackers were in front of us. Why the provost, uh, that driver had not kept moving and had a weapon ready before they was on us means only one of two things."

The captain glowed with Garadon's story-telling.

Time interrupted. "Either he was sleeping, too, or he was part of it."

Garadon's spell on the captain was broken, and he lost interest immediately.

"Yes, of course. The other," sniff and a yawn, "soldiers have established your speed and courage, both of you." Sniff. "Well." Sniff.

"I did collect your weapons, boys." The sergeant spoke clearly, but as he was twenty years younger than Time it did not enhance his authority beyond his muscled torso and arms. Time jumped at it.

"Thank you, sergeant. Are we dismissed, sir?"

"Yes." Sniff. "These forays into Charleston have ended for you two, however." Sniff. "You'll be leaving with two assembled companies," sniff, "of two hundred volunteers and joining General," sniff, "Bragg's army in Tennessee."

Garadon was grinning even wider now. "When?"

"Tomorrow." Sniff. "Go kill some Yankees, not just," sniff, "common thieves. Dismissed." With a wave of the quill feather, the soldiers retreated.

Corporals Time and Garadon had struck up an unlikely friendship months before. Time did not enjoy the company of others for the sake of it, preferring to work independently and lose himself in his thoughts. Garadon enjoyed the give and take of normal human discourse, and was inclined to do less, not more, and would not hesitate to enjoy a privilege, or take it if it fancied him.

What they did have in common was a dedication, Time's newfound and Garadon's inbred, for soldiering. Both were skilled marksmen, whether rifle, pistol, bow, or fishing spear. Both had hands like stone, and were confident and fast in using them. Both instinctively knew and always practiced that getting the final blow in the clinch was an absolute. It was the willingness to end any confrontation with brutal consequences that kept others at bay, and kept them both alive. Neither one worried about living, so approaching death did not deter their enthusiasm for getting close in to finish a fight.

The route from Charleston to south of Nashville, Tennessee, to join Bragg's Army was over 500 miles of mixed road. Wagons were available for supplies and weapons and tenting, so the soldiers would be moving by foot, grumbling all the while that large cannons and munitions went by rail. Most of the volunteers were itinerant poor folk, those not already attached to a unit or having moved north or west, and the professionalism of the two companies was limited by no real training and even less leadership. The overland route north to Tennessee would have too many hills, so the order of march would take the companies of irregulars north to Columbia, South Carolina, then due west around Atlanta, then north again. The dandy captain was nowhere in sight, nor was his sergeant. There were six total officers, all riding horses, who chatted amiably amongst themselves, and stopped for their own respite or pleasure but otherwise had little interaction with the human cattle herd of soldiers, who trudged on foot, poorly equipped, but with mighty hearts. To go to war to fight for their state, the confederacy, for their way of life: a way of life few knew. Laborers all, none had ever, or would ever, own a slave.

The green and brown pine needles of South Carolina yielded to the red clay of Georgia. At nearly twenty miles a day of hard marching with light packs and weapons two companies of one hundred men each from Charleston would be just north of Chattanooga in a little over five weeks, barring a calamity. Three soldiers were mustered out due to foot injury too complicated to remedy. Two deserted. One died of heat stroke. Two of the officers were away without apparent permission for a week as the companies moved around Atlanta, but there was no one senior to hold them accountable. They returned with enough contraband in liquor and tobacco to keep the other four officers happy.

Time and Garadon inadvertently filled the leadership vacuum.

Soldiers will carry only what they are forced to carry. A soldier on the march will dump canteens of water and a day's rations to lighten his load. A soldier on foot will only change his socks if forced to do so under grave threats. The only thing a soldier will cling to, without fail, is his rifle.

The humidity and heat during the summer was more than oppressive. It was monstrous. Time and Garadon took turns leading the entire formation, or trailing it to encourage stragglers. The officers, gentlemen in name only, were useless and knew nothing about moving armed men on foot over hundreds of miles. The first day was all Time needed to establish himself to the companies, and

Garadon's quick insight and enthusiastic support confirmed the leadership shift.

The wagon ambush and the jail-birds' gun play was legendary amongst the volunteers before they moved out of the county north of Charleston.

Time kept to regular breaks, water rations, shirts and coats worn and hats on heads to repel the sun. He forced the changing of available socks, secured the purchase of more for those with only one pair, and supervised the cutting of blisters and the use of grease to smooth a rough boot insole. He occasionally sang aloud, dropping back into the middle of the two-column march, and when shaded the whole company in earshot would respond lustily. On two occasions the men could not continue, when the rain was so murderous that they couldn't see and when the bugs were so thick they could not breathe. "*God Bless our tents*" was the cry during the day-long deluge, and "*God Bless the Chattahoochee*" was the prayer when the insects infested their march.

Twenty miles, give or take, every day for five weeks. One burial, which only extended a noon meal by the time it took to dig the grave and mark it. After a week the soldier's name was forgotten, the only testaments to his life was the plug of tobacco taken by the man who did the most digging, and an unfinished letter addressed to a "Miss Becky" with no address, tear stained, begging her to wait for him.

North of Atlanta, the humidity of the summer's day and the march gave way to a delightful cloudless evening, cool with a breeze from the north Georgia mountains, making for an easy night of gambling, talk, fires, and idleness sprinkled with lofty music that echoed through the trees. The dead straggler had rallied the soldiers, and they now saw themselves as part of real companies of survivors. Good leadership can encourage and exploit that esprit through example, while poor leadership can just as quickly destroy any semblance of martial teamwork.

In Time and Garadon, the two companies had good leadership. With the assistance and remarkable obedience of several other younger non-commissioned officers, Time had established himself as a non-com who cared about his men and could accomplish the mission. Everyone recognized this, and no one was less amazed than Garadon. They sat by themselves at their own fire, segregated from the others, one with plenty of dry wood stacked nearby, courtesy of the initiative of grateful soldiers. Garadon fussed with coffee, trying to avoid the flames while not abandoning the red hot pot.

"Time."

"Yeah."

They spent hours like this each night for over a month. They were the last two to sit, supervising where tents were struck and fires were placed, and conscious of soldier comfort and landowner rights. Occasionally small gestures of appreciation would come their way, like ripe wild berries, or a fiddle concert performed by school children, and one night with fresh summer flowers delivered by two most attentive widows.

"Time, I was thinking, when I met you in Charleston," started Garadon, still struggling with the coffee pot.

"Yeah, I remember."

"I was at one end of that bar, and I saw that you didn't like the people around you. Too loud."

"Yeah, but I don't recall that."

"Right. Well, after you taught them boys some manners; uh, very quick of you, too," Garadon raised his head to meet Time's idle stare, "I saw you as just a killer, one of the bad folk I knew all my life, and stayed clear of."

"Listen, Garadon, I've seen you fight, too. Pretty good at it. You get close, no fear."

"That's not my point, Time."

"Out with it, then."

"A killer doesn't lead men like this. A killer can't care about anything but hisself, himself. You're a Yankee, I know. But you're not a Union man. I'm thinking," Garadon pretended the pot needed attention, and *ouched* with it, "That you were an officer, once. Regular army." He said this casually and evenly and not as an accusation, but as a fact.

"And you'd be wrong." Time acted bored, yet couldn't resist a smile.

Garadon took it as a taunt. "Then where'd you learn this, this stewardship? We are following *you*, Mr. Time. You didn't get this drinking rum in the Caribbean!"

Time fixed Garadon with a stare, and marveled at how much the younger man was perspiring in the cooling night so close to the heat, how the flicking tongues from the fire gave his angry glare more gravity than his spoken words.

"I'll tell you, Garadon. Just you. Can't make a bigger deal out of it than it should be. Back in '47, I was working in Tennessee and a regiment was being mustered to go to Mexico."

"I remember, but I was just a boy."

"Yeah. I wasn't. I joined 'em. Volunteers all. We set out on foot for Vera Cruz in November, then Mexico City in December, but by then the fighting was over. We lost a hundred men of the thousand we started with, mostly to sickness, some to stupid. Each one pained our commanding officer, a political appointee, and even though he showed it he didn't let it distract him. A prince of a man."

"Even officers have good men among 'em."

Time stretched, now expansive in recalling details, the memory of almost fifteen years before dancing behind his moist eyes. "Yeah. Yeah, they do. We stayed in Mexico until '48, and were back in Louisville by July and they disbanded us by the end of the month. That was my army career."

"You were an officer, right?"

"No. A private. But our regimental commander was a young man, about my age then. He walked more than he rode. He forced breaks for water and socks and knew what chafing and rawness was, yeah, he did. He cared. He tasked us all, made us march every hour of light and many hours without, but we knew that if he could do it, we could do it. I learned a lot just from watching him. He was a damn good officer. I'd follow him into hell."

"Think he's still alive?"

"I know he is. So do you. John Breckinridge, the vice president; was, that is. Now Major General. With any luck we'll be in his command."

@@@

After five weeks, the two companies made contact with Confederate troops outside of Tullahoma, Tennessee. The last four days it rained with a fury, and the esprit developing in the irregular companies was exchanged for the wet noise of angry men bristling to do anything to assuage their individual discomfort and their collective cynicism. One of the officers saw fit to cut a switch to motivate the men to look smarter on the march approaching the command post headquarters of General Braxton Bragg. A soldier reached out, grabbed the swinging rod on the down stroke, and hit the officer's horse with a rage that sent the steed at a full gallop and the officer screaming for the beast to yield.

Bragg and Breckinridge watched the small spectacle with silent amusement from under the senior Bragg's field tent.

"I can find a use for some of these men, general," said Breckinridge, absently, his clear blue eyes arching slightly, his bearing as impressive as ever.

"You shall. We can't keep that group together. They're volunteers, John. You may use a heavy hand in dealing with them."

Breckinridge's countenance hid his disdain for the implication. "Of course, general."

@@@

2
Cloud's family

The boys were running through the brush, knowing it by rote more than instinct, where the wood was dense and what to avoid, confident their foot-strikes would be true.

They were slowed by the burden of carrying rifles and ammunition, and small bundles of food stolen from the Yankee encampment.

Where the boys ran free of error, the Yankee soldier could only make false steps and stumbles. The soldier was not gaining ground, and the farther he chased, the more likely he would be lost.

Adam and Goff propelled themselves, running faster as the cries of exertion and threats from the Yankee became less distinct. The soldier's footfalls were muffled by his cries of pain as he ran headlong into the thicket, guessing the direction of the boys who stole four rifles, powder and balls, and precious hardtack.

The soldier's fear of the consequence of having the stacked arms in his care stolen so brazenly in the sinking afternoon sun was greater than being lost forever in the Tennessee wilderness.

He could no longer see the brush move where the boys had been, sweat streaking his vision, but he could hear them.

The boys, brothers, had reached a shallow creek, and the taller one, Adam, stumbled, and splashed too loudly. They did not hesitate further, now sprinting up the opposite embankment, all familiar to them, knowing the root knots and rocks that made the climb easy, even with a burden. A pursuer would struggle.

"Where have you been?" A gangly girl, taller and older than the boys, with the same light brown hair as both lads. Hers was tied back severely, and her small aquiline nose flared in anger over a petite mouth with small even teeth. At 18 years old, her promise of beauty into womanhood was overshadowed by her instinct to scold and protect the boys, and she noticed for the first time what her brothers were carrying. Her eyes flashed bright green.

"Genny, we're being chased by a Yankee," barked Adam.

"Oh no! He'll shoot you both!"

The husky brother, Goff, coughed a laugh, scrambling up the hill.

"We have his weapon, and others. He can't shoot us!"

"Oh, oh, no! I can hear him crashing in the trees – run, run!"

They dove into the brush and disappeared, now soundless.

The Yankee hurtled himself through the wood, and smashed halfway through the stream, heaving and panicked. He stopped and gazed up the opposite slope, and saw a pretty girl standing at the top of the bank, hands on hips.

"Where did they go," he gasped.

"Who?"

"Two or three, they have my rifle, and others." He spread his arms wide, his eyes even wider. "Which way?" A plea.

Genny smiled. This Yankee soldier was not much older than her brothers, about her age.

"Two or three what?" She reached behind her head and undid the ribbon holding her hair back, and the long wavy locks fell over her shoulders and chest as she shook her head to loosen it. "What's your name?" She asked, a subtle flirt.

"What? What?" The soldier's concentration was quickly unfocused. She looked like his girl back home. She radiated warmth and coolness at the same time, as his soaked feet started to numb in the middle of the stream. Her smile finished him.

"I'm Genevieve." She sat at the top of the embankment, still smiling, smoothing her long skirt around her.

He knew his pursuit was now useless.

She knew her brothers may escape, for now.

"I'm Stevie." He hung his head in fatigue and resignation. "I was a soldier." He walked up to the girl, smiling at her in return, unbuttoning his coat, the warmth of the late August sun crisscrossing through the trees and touching his eyes to a squint.

@@@

Adam and Goff Moas made it to the thatched wooden hut long minutes later, breathless.

"We need to go back for Genny," cried Goff.

"She doesn't need us. We hide the guns, first."

The hut was spartan and clean, but missing most comforts of a home, except books. The soft feminine touches were absent, most sold long ago. Used burlap and flannel pieces, scraps from foraging around the Confederate camps, were in a pile by the door, sufficient to wrap the stolen rifles. Adam took all four out to a large fallen tree fifty yards from the one room house. The privy and outdoor oven were in the opposite direction on a more beaten path. The hollowed out trunk was sitting in dense brush, and served as a perfect hideaway for the stolen weapons.

At the hut Goff removed one of the floor planks near the single door. An iron box was already firmly placed in the hole; Goff opened it, placed the ammunition inside, and replaced the floor board.

A shadow crossed in front of Goff. Initially startled, he relaxed as he recognized a young woman's scent.

"Take nothing out of there, young man."

"Hey, Cloud. I'm putting bullets and such into it, see?" Goff smiled up at the girl.

Dressed nearly identical to Genevieve, the black girl wore a bonnet to cover her short hair. Hands on hips, she nearly spat at the younger boy kneeling in the doorway. She thrust an accusatory finger at his head.

"What have you done, now?"

Adam came up quickly behind her.

"We caught a Union sentry napping about four, five miles from here. We were looking for food, Cloud, honest."

"And the rifles were by a pack with ammunition and bread and all that..." Goff pointed to the small table centered in the hut, with scraps from the theft.

"And we didn't see anyone, and the soldier was asleep. We grabbed everything and ran."

Cloud was fuming, "Why rifles? They won't give up looking for rifles! Everyone steals food, but not, not their weapons! And so close! They'll find us, kill you, and Lord knows what will happen to Miss Genny!"

The boys hung their heads. Adam spoke without meeting her eye.

"We met her at the creek, where we bathe, you know, where we find minnows and frogs and..."

Cloud cut him off. "What happened?" Evenly, without emotion.

Goff spoke up.

"We kept running. I think Gen stayed to delay the soldier. He didn't follow us."

"I'll go see to her. You two take everything to outside of Jackson's encampment. Do it now. Everything you can carry."

"Why?"

"We need protection, now, more than our freedom. I'll find Miss Genny."

"We can't carry everything." A whine.

"You'll carry all of it. Leave the bedding, I'll get it later."

"But it's getting late, and it'll be colder soon. Without this house..."

"Boys, we won't make it through the night, let alone September. The winter will be on us, soon enough. We need the soldiers now." Cloud wiped her brow in concern.

"What about you?"

"You know what to tell people, now get to work, there's no time to lose. I must find Genny." With that pronounced, Cloud charged into the woods for the creek, and she thought of how much she feared for losing her friend, and how much she owed the Moas family.

@@@

The four teens, Genevieve and her brothers Adam and Goff, and the Negro Cloud Parker, had found the thatched wood hut months earlier in the late spring of 1862, after wandering around north Georgia for almost a year after the sudden deaths of their parents, Abel and Kandice Moas. But for the Grace of God and the slave Cloud's judgment, they may have been murdered on the path northward.

The Moas family had lived for over a decade in quiet comfort hard earned. Abel Moas had been a teamster in high demand, and he drove all sizes of teams of horses, donkeys, or oxen from the Tennessee border to Atlanta and its environs. It was steady work, physically demanding, but the good pay sustained his family's simple life in the hills. His wife, Kandice, was a bookish sort and devoted mother who indulged her eldest and only daughter, Genevieve, two things: good books, and the girl Cloud. How Cloud Parker came to be a member of their family was never discussed. It was assumed.

Cloud recalled only being led away from her family by Abel Moas when she was six; she had just had a birthday. Her mother's face was strained, and her brother Henry cried, even though he was several years older than Cloud and tall like a man.

Cloud Parker was neither the Moas' slave nor servant. When the curious inquired how a modest family could keep a servant, they were told she was their property and that was their business alone. No one challenged Abel Moas, and Kandice was always so sunny and pleasant and warm that the nosy simply smiled and nodded assent.

Both girls, Genny and Cloud, were born the same year —1845— hundreds of miles apart, worlds away from each other, connected only by the desperation of living that comes from always being poor. Their blossoming womanhood was just as different. Genevieve was tall, pretty, delicate, vivacious, and happy to know everyone. Cloud was small but intensely strong, as dark as Genny was light, and she rarely smiled. She trusted no one. Both benefited from Kandice's constant tutelage in literature, poetry, and polemics from early on. Both proved remarkable students, hungry for the written word and the forests of books to be explored, learning at the knee of one who loved reading second only to her bright girls. As different as the girls were in physical stature and temperament, they were bonded as closely as sisters could be, without jealousy, pettiness, or cynicism. Kandice would not allow it.

They loved the challenge of each other's insight, and their differences blended. Genny and Cloud never had a cross word to the other, and were devoted to each other.

And they had their work, or "distractions" as they called them in jest.

Genny's work was the boys. Four years her junior, the twins Adam and Gosford were opposites to themselves, too, but just as devoted. Adam was tall, nearly as tall as his father Abel, but lanky like Kandice and Genny, and they shared the same small down-turned nose. Adam was always the first to speak, and did not share his mother's passion for an education. Only seeking his father's approval, Adam wanted to be a teamster.

Gosford had his father's broad shoulders, which developed early. He was called Goff since he could first write, about seven years earlier. He consistently omitted the "s" when writing his name, and all six of them would laugh good-naturedly. Abel suggested that Gosford didn't like his name, so perhaps he should be called Goff.

A nickname at such a young age was a powerful inducement, especially if the child had a hand in it. The family, and Cloud at that age was every bit a part of the Moas family, called him Goff forevermore, except Kandice, who had named her children with precision and thought Gosford was a most lovely one.

After Kandice died, no one ever knew him as anyone other than Goff.

Cloud's work was manifold. Constant companion to Genny, except when she was minding the boys, Cloud helped Kandice with all the little things of survival as a family bound to be self-sufficient. Kandice needed help with gathering and preparation and cleaning and mending and skinning and hygiene. Kandice spent more time with Cloud than her own daughter. She saw herself as an educator, and the girls as gifted, though Cloud's curiosity to learn eclipsed Genny's ability early on. Genny worked hard at her lessons, but Cloud grasped things the first time, with real understanding. If one girl wasn't present, there would be no lesson, as Kandice was acutely aware of favoritism. She treated Cloud as a daughter, and that was that.

During those early years when Abel was home, about one week a month, Cloud would follow him, and he would teach and philosophize about beasts of burden, their care, how to speak to them, how to care enough for them that they would carry any load with steady confidence or walk off a cliff if required to do so. Even though Abel was a simple, hard-working man, he always had one sound horse for himself, and one for Kandice. He traded them when a bargain suited him, and the infrequent visitor or more frequent travel acquaintance knew that Abel Moas was a man of integrity. If it came to horses, men sought Abel.

When it came to gambling, Abel sought men. The Moas family always had what it needed, but never saved anything, except books. Abel Moas never drank and never smoked, but he could not pass a card game without taking a seat. He told Kandice he won more than he lost, but she knew that dumb luck was the only thing keeping them alive.

That luck brought Cloud Parker to them in 1850. A wager won.

The family's luck ran out in 1861. Both Abel and Kandice passed away within a week of each other, of a fever that could not be quenched. A year later the orphaned children and Cloud were living on the periphery of poor rural society, in a makeshift hut in Tennessee.

@@@

Cloud half ran through the brush, taking the route she always took to the bend in the creek where it pooled enough to sit and bathe. It was getting too cool to sit there for long now, and her concern for Genny's safety was exceeded only by her curiosity on why Genny had ventured there alone. Perhaps she sensed the boys' trouble, she thought.

She prayed as she ran. Cloud did not believe in spirits generally, but she did have the Moases' unshakeable faith in the Resurrection. She could not run faster. Her shoes were too worn, and her heels were constantly blistered.

Many long minutes later she could see the rise before the creek, and Genny lying on her back, arms wide.

"Oh, dear Genny! God help me!" Cloud sprinted to Genny, fearing the worst, and just as she was about to throw herself at the motionless girl, Genny sat up, and smiled.

"Cloud! You startled me!"

Cloud caught her breath, fists on hips. "I... startled you?"

"Yes! Where are the boys?"

"The boys? They're fine. Was there a soldier through here? A Yankee?"

Genny smiled. "Yes, but he's gone back from where he came, I think. Stevie. As cute a boy as I have ever seen." She looked skyward, and fidgeted where she sat, smoothing her skirt constantly.

"Genny, we can't stay here, the soldiers may be looking for the stolen weapons. We can't stay here. They'll question your soldier-boy and come looking..."

"Oh, I don't know. I think Stevie loves me."

Cloud shook her head, sat down next to her only friend, and told her the plan.

@@@

September was cool but dry. As the leaves died the air grew thinner, and the temperature swing between dawn, midday and dusk became more pronounced. Genevieve and Cloud and the boys remained on the periphery of the Confederate brigades, the girls doing horse work for soldiers, gladly. The boys sought others like themselves, boys too young to serve but eager to prove their manhood. Tenting was given to them by the Rebel quartermaster, as they provided some valuable intelligence about the relative strength and assumed weakness of the nearby Union forces. The Moas family remained in the shadows of armed men and materiel, some off to Nashville, some to Chattanooga, some to mass east of Murfreesboro, though the majority moved north to central Kentucky. Cloud barely spoke and was assumed to be the property of Genevieve. The pretense was easy for them both. Cloud doted on Genny, Genny wanted a friend, and no one suspected anything untoward about the relationship.

The boys knew better, but loved Cloud as they loved their sister. It never crossed their mind to say other than the girl Cloud Parker was a slave and had always been their property.

3
Breckinridge

By the late summer and early autumn of 1862, the confederacy, emboldened by necessity, took the initiative to invade Kentucky to obtain supplies and wreak havoc with the Union army's complacency. After successful forays deep into the state, recruitment increased and morale blossomed for the Rebels. Kentucky remained divided politically, and the official position of neutrality of a year earlier died quickly. Both the nascent confederacy and the struggling parent of the United States had stars on their respective flags claiming Kentucky as their own. In spite of its many recent successes, Confederate commanders fought amongst themselves, their respective egos being greater than their collective good judgment.

It was into this cauldron of attack and defend, internal pettiness, and run and attack by maneuver and surprise, that the Union and Confederate forces fought in every imaginable savagery, from skirmishes to set piece battles, threatening and causing severe devastation in a desperate bid for survival, or better, victory.

The arc of history is most often altered by the consequences caused by the decisions of men, however flawed in character. Great and grave changes in life may occur as a thunderclap, unbidden in shock and surprise, unerringly with cataclysmic results. Even greater changes in mankind's existence happen as a result of the slow and inexorable forces of nature, like the incessant drip-drip-drip of water on a stone never noticed when forced to the surface over a millennium earlier, the drops unhurriedly hollowing out the rock, creating a pool, a small reservoir that freezes in winter and sends one unsuspecting person slipping on the ice. Fate.

Forces of nature are always stronger than man, but not always the will of determined men. Fate, to the emboldened, the committed, and the resolute, is a consequence of preparation and prayer, a gift that spells both an end and a beginning.

Ambition is an ugly mistress.

Major General John C. Breckinridge had resigned from the U.S. Senate representing Kentucky less than a year before, having left the vice-presidency of the United States six months prior to that. The youngest U.S. Vice President up that point in her history, he was elected with James Buchanan in 1856, when he was 35 years old.

And she can be fickle.

Breckinridge always had a deep affinity toward the political class, and he was a natural at living up to its expectations. His family had roots and connections going back to his grandfather's service in Thomas Jefferson's cabinet.

He earned a bachelor's degree in 1838, at 17 years old, and began the study of law the following year, receiving his law degree and license to practice in February 1841. He had just turned 20, and from the outset identified himself as a Democrat. Breckinridge married in 1843, began a family, and solidified his ties with future senators and statesmen. He worked steadily, without scandal or distinction. He supported the Mexican/American War, and was appointed a major of the Third Kentucky Regiment in September of 1847.

Myth-making after the dust of heroes and villains have receded or been drained away by the erosion of time is common and appreciated by most, even if improbable.

And she can cause great pain in every step.

The true acts, the small ones, do give a glimpse as to why, perhaps, a single man can capture the light of fortune to his circumstance with the shadow of impending ruptures of history.

The Third Kentucky set out for Vera Cruz the first of November 1847, arriving by the end of the month, a journey of over 1,000 miles. Officers of high rank always rode a horse, but the young and fit Breckinridge walked all but two days, allowing weary and infirm soldiers the chance to recuperate by riding. The gesture was not unnoticed and was long remembered by fighting men from Kentucky.

And she assumes uglier hand maidens and courtiers, for the glow of adulation can never stray from her bitter intensity.

The Third never contributed to the subjugation of Mexican bandits, although nearly ten percent of the soldiers succumbed mortally to illness. Breckinridge served honorably but without heroism, and his political star remained in a steady, if gentle, ascendancy. A slave owner himself, he tread skillfully with political and religious factions and churches which opposed the "peculiar" institution in official terms. His ability to look at a broad view in respect to the repugnance of slavery, doing one thing and saying another, made him an ideal compromise candidate for many. Breckinridge possessed a natural political charisma and his strong voice and youth stirred a young nation still bursting with the enthusiasm of knowing that freedom is best exercised with vigor.

And she may choose the reluctant beau before he can escape her promise, her charms...

He cultivated, with deliberate and appropriate modesty, a strong personal relationship with the mythic Henry Clay. Before the Mexico campaign, Breckinridge had delivered a moving eulogy at the memorial service for many of Kentucky's fallen, which included the mighty Clay's son. The oration so moved Clay that he unashamedly wept. A few years later, as the aging Clay rested before his well-earned eternal reward, Breckinridge visited him daily in Lexington.

When the great statesman of the era passed on, the youthful first term congressman, only 31 years old in 1852, was chosen to deliver the eulogy. His personal favor with the legendary and popular Clay, his eulogy for the formidable statesman at the next congressional session, and his uncanny touch in not offending but inspiring, secured the appearance of John C. Breckinridge as the heir to Henry Clay's grass roots populism.

And she surprises both with her disappointments and delights.

The two term congressman, barely 35 years old, after a fractious and raucous nominating process that he demurred to at first, and artfully succumbed to at last, became the Democratic vice presidential nominee in 1856. Breckinridge's strength was his oratorical skill, and he enjoyed the campaign as much as he enjoyed the people he sought to serve.

He and James Buchanan won.

Although he maintained cordial relations with President Buchanan, he strengthened his connections in congress, the senate he presided over, and his home state of Kentucky, so much so that even though his vice presidential term had not ended, the Kentucky General Assembly chose him as the successor to its current U.S. Senator, who would leave office in 1861. The odd convolutions of procedural politics, the senate's Byzantine and flawed rules notwithstanding, elevated a sitting vice president with a built-in seat in the august body he currently presided over. This was viewed with no more than a yawn.

And her perfume is like currency, heady and intoxicating, lingering only in proximity to her...

Breckinridge's ultimate mistress, his quiet ambition, had one more test of him.

In 1860 the election for president was seemingly his to lose as the sitting vice president. The complications of unplanned public discontent, largely a slavery issue, divided the nation. It also divided the parties internally, and four candidates ran aggressive, venomous campaigns. America's history has been indelibly shaped by the election of Lincoln, and Breckinridge was always acutely aware that he placed second in the Electoral College, with virtually the same electors as the combined total of the third and fourth finishers, Bell and Douglas. Breckinridge's popular vote total of over 18 percent was provided largely by the rural area of the Deep South, independent men, not slave owners.

And she would abandon one who loses.

The darkening shadow of the inevitable conflict clouded the rising star. John C. Breckinridge favored the Dred Scott decision, an appalling stain on the U.S. Supreme Court's legacy, and he predicted violent resistance even as he strenuously advocated against secession. As states bolted from the Union, the senator from Kentucky could see clearly the path he came from, and to where it would lead him.

And she seduces the ambitious to his end, unloved and reviled, for he could not live up to his own lofty goals.

In August of 1861, no longer vice president and now serving Kentucky as its U.S. Senator, Breckinridge declared his allegiance to the notion of the confederacy. In September the Kentucky state legislation requested his resignation from the U.S. Senate. In a letter to the people of Kentucky, as a public pronouncement, Breckinridge stated that the Union (now fractured) no longer existed, and his sympathies lie with the southern cause. He'd rather give up his senate seat for the musket of a soldier, he declared, and was summarily indicted for treason in November and condemned as a traitor in December by a unanimous, albeit shrunken, U.S. Senate. He joined two other senators who had been expelled earlier in '61.

And she touches his arm with one last wonderful chance at redemption, to win her favor, however small...

Before his condemnation he was appointed a Brigadier General in the Confederate Army and given a command where he trained a composite force of Kentuckians, affectionately and loosely called the Orphan Brigade. Major General John Breckinridge led well, was wounded, and remained a vital commander through engagements at Shiloh and Vicksburg and Baton Rouge. The distinction of meritorious and heroic service was proven. He earned it.

And she makes jealous others who will do his dreams of redemption great harm.

By December of 1862, General Braxton Bragg showed the Confederate Army in general, and his subordinate John Breckinridge in particular, what mulish incompetency was all about.

@@@

The Confederate camp had the slow sounds of fatigue rippling through the tents, the sighs and barks of men in boredom, the edgy whine of horses baying and fussing. Fires cracked. The scent of coffee and burning wood mixed with the stench of human sweat and grease.

The burning wood, wet and smoky, always won out.

Breckinridge's command tent was simple, and this morning he sat on an armless wooden chair facing the maps strewn on the table in front of him. His staff adjutants had more spacious quarters, an indulgence he silently encouraged. His years as Vice President brought him more pampering than he could endure, and although he allowed flattery to soften him, he was determined to be a rock in the field with his men.

His bravery and military skill was never truly in doubt, as he had been tested in both his tender youth and his maturity. At 42 years he felt the sharp pain of age yet vowed silently to keep his discomfort to himself. He stretched his legs out, and raised his arms high over his head. Breckinridge enjoyed the few minutes afforded him in solitude.

"General."

"Yes."

A gaunt captain entered the tent. As old as his general, this captain was an effective aide, and had a unique skill set that Breckinridge admittedly lacked. The captain was a student at West Point years before, but was not offered a commission due to a recurrent leg injury. Captain Dayton was more experienced and qualified than his superiors in some respects, but could not serve actively until the war started. Even then the North would not take him.

He sought and secured a commission in the confederacy, and he never wavered in his own conviction of moral right. Dayton would show his mettle. The Confederate command knew that this northerner had much intimate knowledge of geography and urban culture that eluded their own intelligence. Dayton had piles of tact and he could fill the breach in intelligence. He had a skill for administration and was steady and spare with advice. Breckinridge valued his word and military acumen, and trusted it, almost, without question.

Dayton's only ambition was to prove his value.

Breckinridge only wanted it all to end, knowing that a return to Washington, DC, would never be. He feared the end of the Union, and a spiral into chaos for generations to come. The great experiment of a democratic republic might come to a dispiriting end. But, if a second republic, a confederacy, could hold, God willing, he could lead that new nation.

"Sir, the 6th. Poorly formed, mostly irregulars. There's one company that is all, nearly all, just in their mid-teens. And younger."

The 6th was cobbled together from volunteers who hailed from Kentucky. Called "orphans" by the press, their own leadership, and even amongst themselves, the "Orphan Brigade" was a political moniker: the state of Kentucky was both slave and free and allegiance was a matter of personal conscience. The Orphan Brigade was proud of their ability which rested almost entirely on a perceived courage in the face of overwhelming pressure to side with the Union.

One of the bitterest ironies of the confederacy was that most of the enlisted men never owned a slave, or even aspired to, but were willing to fight and die so the wealthy might enjoy their own notion of freedom, their way of life.

"The 6th Regiment is part of Hansen's Brigade." Breckinridge had a capacity for detail and needed to subtly remind this captain of that fact. "I think there are six companies in that regiment, barely over five hundred men. They've had a devil of a time coming up with more volunteers."

"Sir, it's to remain six companies, sir. Colonel Lewis is forming all the youngest and greenest into G Company, augmenting its strength. I wish to discuss this situation with you, sir."

The excessive deference was unusual for this captain, and it concerned Breckinridge. He met Dayton's hollow stare. He knew the captain was not political. There must be a compelling concern, he thought.

"Of course, captain. Out with it."

"Sir, I am not questioning the good colonel. He sees G Company as a reserve unit. I do see the intent and merit. But our field leadership is raw and only partially tested."

Breckinridge tired easily of the obvious. Four years in Washington will inure one to the necessity of apologizing and asserting simultaneously, he thought, but that did not detract from the boredom.

"Speak plainly, captain, I know all this."

"Sir, there's a corporal, an older soldier, about my age. He has been with Lewis, Colonel Lewis, since the middle of this summer, came with the Charleston irregulars on foot. He's a fighter, a natural leader in battle. He is respected for his knowledge."

"And you want him commissioned. Why wouldn't Colonel Lewis or Brigadier General Hanson ask me outright?" It was difficult for Breckinridge to hide his irritation.

"He's a northerner, sir. He finds this enterprise, our war, in a most foul humor. But he fights like the devil, and men respond to him."

Breckinridge saw the problems quickly. A northerner, like Dayton, fighting for the South was not uncommon. But this other man could be a criminal, and the army had enough problems. His lack of pedigree was a formidable drawback. The morale of the other officers and self-important soldiers and hangers-on would have to be taken into account. It was good to flush this out with Dayton. Whenever Breckinridge spoke to the other generals or field grade officers he was expected to be the political voice in the room. With Dayton, here and now, they could chop through pros and cons without it being recorded for posterity.

"I see. Well. We can't very well give a corporal command of a company."

"Sir, if we designate G Company as a reserve company, for volunteers without experience, then they are recruits under the command of training. And he'll command only a platoon."

"And we make your northern devil provide the instruction in garrison."

"Yes, sir. He would rise to it, sir. I have heard of his vitality in close combat and he could train the... children."

Breckinridge blanched when he heard this reference. But it was accurate. So many children, true orphans of the rural south.

"All in their teens?"

"Sir, certainly all bare-faced. There are over one hundred who are years away from a razor, and some could pass for girls except they are always filthy."

The general smiled, which turned to a pained expression, and shook his head.

"Our children will die for this, this." He stared blankly at his boots. "What's this corporal's name?"

"Time, sir. James Time."

"The name sounds familiar," he paused. "We'll make him a sergeant tomorrow. Muster the commanders for me, Captain Dayton. I think I'll review everyone's plan for reserve companies, everyone's orphans."

@@@

4

Orphans, All

The Moas family, all orphans in their own right, and Cloud Parker, a free woman without the documentation to prove it, were struggling to find a place for themselves amongst the shifting tides of warring armies and their men, horses, weaponry and materiel in central Tennessee in the fall of 1862.

Genevieve and Cloud sewed and mended anything and everything, securing by mid-October a tent large enough for four to sleep comfortably, and for two people to sit at a table during the day and work in privacy. The women, girls still for the most part, decided the best course was to stay close to the command posts of the Confederate army. After the encounter with the Union soldier, they knew Adam and Goff would not be able to harness their impulses to steal for bounty or food. The girls could barely control themselves.

The boys were vigorous in finding scrap, cleaning weapons for pennies, or performing the most menial and undignified work in a soldier's life: digging, cleaning, and burying latrines.

Though average in stature, both Adam and Goff possessed hard hands and an indomitable energy, never lagging in motion from sun-up to sundown. They missed their parents desperately, but did enjoy the freedom that comes with random encounters and no accountability, always assured that they had each other's back. If the warm fluttering of feminine nesting was their need at the hour, they knew their sister and step-sister (as they saw Cloud) would indulge the desire to be pampered and fussed over. Goff thought it a perfect life.

Adam was hungry for more. The war was on, and he knew that there would be no future if they could not account for themselves as men.

"We'll be boot-lickers all our lives if we don't volunteer!" Adam beseeched the tent-top early one evening.

"But you're too young! You could be killed!" shrieked Genevieve, much too loudly.

"We'll starve at this rate, Genny. If we join, then we'll get pay and you can live better," reasoned Goff.

"It's all you can do to keep the tent patched, Genny. We'd be on our own. You needn't worry, we'd be with the army!" Adam stated it as though all their troubles would end in a flash.

Cloud interjected quietly, her voice trailing off, "And we may need to leave soon, Genny."

The unspoken drama of their situation was not one of food, or homelessness, or being orphaned without resources. It was Cloud's status. The murmurs of her not being Genevieve's property were louder than ever, and was one of the reasons the Moases avoided the civilian population, as poor as it was in that country. Miss Genny works as hard as the darkie, they said, with venom and skepticism. What kind of servant is this Cloud Parker? What kind of mistress is this Genevieve?

"I think we should stay near the soldiers for the winter, Cloud. There's nowhere to run."

A rustle at the tent flap, and a polite cough.

"We heard a scream. Are you all right, miss?"

The four stared at each other. At night, they were never bothered. The lack of a fire implied they retired for the evening. Their hesitation was too long.

"I will see for myself, then," said Time, as he entered the tent, which suddenly became too small for everyone. Garadon stuck in his head only, saw Genny, smiled, and removed his hat.

"Well. Evening, Miss." Garadon's toothy smile was like the sun in the flickering candlelight.

Time saw in an instant the scream was either a game or a family squabble, and the squabble looked to win out as he surveyed the faces for further information. The stricken look on the girls, both of them, though different in intensity, made the same statement. They were afraid, and their posture showed fear of soldiers in general

Time took charge. "It's cold tonight. We'll make a fire. We need to talk." His manner was paternal, not predatory, and all, especially Cloud, sensed it. She met his eye.

Time looked back and forth at Adam and Goff. "Gather more wood, boys. Missy," he said to Cloud, "I'll have some coffee."

@@@

The fire was smoky, but the absence of wind drew the gray and white upwards, randomly touching the circle of six. Quarters were tight in their little section of the woods, and they sat close to each other, which matched Time's plan to talk to the group in low tones that would be difficult to overhear.

Genevieve blurted out introductions, their family story, of their parents' deaths almost two years before. Of growing up with Cloud as friend and sister, of the boys stealing guns from Yankees well over a month ago, of abandoning their shack of a home, of being camp followers for pennies, of no papers for Cloud and the fear she'd be stolen and sold or worse, of the boys wanting to join the army and being too, much too young. Even Cloud was in awe of Genny's ability to tell so much so fast, and Time's patience was profound.

"Oh, dear, we love books, too, yes we do!" Genny smiled and clasped her hands under her chin, and Cloud returned the gesture and sentiment with a wan smile and her hand over her chest.

A wisp of smoke rolled toward Genny, and she coughed slightly and fanned the air in front of her.

"Where are the guns?" Garadon asked, sitting next to Genny, as he tried to coax the smoke away from the girl and towards himself.

"Hidden," Cloud answered too quickly, before either of the boys could gather the breath to answer.

"Never mind that, now." Time gave Garadon the slightest of reproachful glances. "Are you all right, Miss Genny? Do you feel well?"

"I'm tired is all, Sergeant Time."

Time had been promoted to sergeant in the 6th Kentucky volunteers, an irregular regiment that was augmented by the companies from South Carolina. The promotion was met with great enthusiasm, officers and men alike, as reward for Time's steady hand in the march to Tennessee and intense skirmishes afterward. But not everyone was enthused, as Garadon harbored a small resentment as he believed his effort merited recognition, too. Time had told him to be patient, and asked Garadon to not seek another unit, telling the disappointed corporal that his time would come, and his strengths were known and appreciated by his friend.

"I understand, Miss Genny. And you, Miss Cloud?" Time discerned a tension unspoken.

"I am well, yes. But Miss Genny has the morning sickness, I believe." Cloud and Genny had not discussed it, and Cloud thought she could trust Time for the moment.

She also wanted both men, and all men by extension, on notice of Genny's condition. Time and Garadon understood her meaning immediately, though the boys did not. Garadon's initial ardor cooled imperceptibly.

"You look an angel, Miss. I pray you feel better," Garadon said with a smoothness and sincerity that brought a spring of hidden tears to both Genny and Cloud. The boys watched open-mouthed.

"I can show you where the rifles are," whispered Adam, "But we want to join the army, too."

Genny and Cloud gasped in unison, for different reasons, Genny in fear of losing the boys, Cloud in fear of losing the weapons.

Garadon inquired through a tendril of smoke, "How many?"

"Four," Goff said, with pride.

"How old are you boys?"

"They're thirteen, barely!" Genny was desperate.

Time scratched his beard, and Garadon gazed peripherally at Genevieve, as much as good manners allowed. Cloud stood up.

"The boys will need rifles, sergeant. And we'll need cash money for the other two. We can't let you simply take them. They are all we have."

"Fine." Garadon took charge, now staring completely at Genny, who returned the gaze. "We'll do right by the boys, and, of course, by you. Rest easy tonight."

Time stood, pausing as if still deciding. "Adam. Goff. Either myself or the corporal will come for you tomorrow, mid-morning." He looked at Genny, then Cloud, then back to Genny.

"They'll always be with me. Always."

@@@

Time ensured his 25 men, all boys, were busy when they should be, and were resting when required. The first few days after mustering the company of one hundred, his commanding officer, a young captain, made Time's platoon know its place.

"Learn from your sergeant. Stay out of the way, otherwise."

Time and Garadon joked that they would probably never see the company commander again; they did, but not with any regularity. Time was even excluded from routine meetings and at first was piqued that he was being ignored by the command, even after explicit instructions from Breckinridge's personal aide. Time had to suffer the indignity of having to receive orders from a runner. Garadon tried to sell Time on the beauty of this.

"No reports except a morning report. None of these boys will get sick unless we tell 'em they're sick. None will desert, because their honor as soldiers is more important than everything except their mommas, and most don't even have that. They're not old enough to know better. About honor, I mean."

"And I can tell a runner to go to hell if I want."

Garadon laughed out loud. "You won't, though."

"But I could." Time, resigned to the assignment, was willing to make the best of a situation he could not control. It made his decision to look after his boys, first and foremost before any mission, that much easier.

Time took to his new charge with a paternal cynicism, never quite concealing his amusement at the seriousness of the young men, the boys, his orphans.

The Moas brothers attracted the smallest of the boys, as their confident familiarity was a beacon of acceptance. Adam and Goff had each other and it made them stand taller.

A rubbery boy kept bragging of his prowess at swimming, and insisted on being called "Fish."

"Well, what's your name?"

"Fish. Because I was the best swimmer. I skim on the water."

"But what's your Christian name? Your given name?" Adam smiled to draw the boy out.

"Fish, I said. Always has been."

Another boy soldier was fascinated with money, though he never had any, and had much difficulty with the concept of paper, precious metals, and simple shiny objects. His name was Billy.

"Why, this is worth a lot! I could trade this for a pig, or a cow, or even a horse! Look, I rub the metal, and, and, it will shine… It will, I haven't done it in a while," Billy's enthusiasm trailed off.

He was rubbing a fork, one of a four-piece cutlery set he looked at often and kept in a tight pouch on his hip. He would take out the pieces, all of them, return three, and then start rubbing the last implement, now a fork, vigorously with whatever was handy, no matter how dirty or ineffective.

"What makes you think someone would give you a horse for tableware?"

"Because it's silver! It is!"

Goff was exasperated. "No it ain't. Doesn't even look like metal!"

"What the heck do *you* know?"

Back and forth Goff and Adam and Fish and Billy would argue and brag, wrestle and what-if together. Boys trying to be manly, worldly, and brave.

"We're not orphans, completely, you know."

"Our parents are good and dead, that's not changing."

"But their name lives on. In us. We know the name, we'll carry it forever. We're never completely orphaned, never completely alone."

"You sound like Genny and Cloud. Stop it."

@@@

Time never liked the trader, the swarthy featured stump of a man with unnaturally dark eyes. An itinerant hawker of all sorts of sundries, Mother Corn pulled a sturdy cart with tobacco, playing cards, sweets, boot laces, socks, and a variety of lotions to soothe or ward off chafing and bug bites. He was popular with soldiers and officers alike, as he laughed quickly at all asides, no matter how raunchy or banal, and had an odd habit of twitching his head mid-sentence, as if hearing a far-off warning to not talk too much. Mother Corn had a ready grin, showing crooked and green teeth, and always arrived clean shaven. He never carried paper or pencil or newsprint, since he bragged that he couldn't read or write and lived by his instincts on what to sell for how much or for what value in trade. Scrupulously fair with all, fawning toward higher ranking officers, Mother Corn was accepted as a normal part of Confederate camp life in the autumn of '62. No one knew where he hailed from or lived, and all just assumed he slept under his wagon away from the garrison or bivouac.

Time refused to engage him, and advised his platoon to do their business with the trader and get back to work without extended conversation. The young orphans were nothing if not obedient, in direct contrast to the saltier Kentuckians who carried themselves with a swagger that feigned confidence. Time's boys avoided the inevitable ring of laughter and gossip that surrounded Mother Corn.

@@@

Adam and Goff often chided each other over the smallest things, but were acutely respectful of each other's fragile and budding manhood. When it came to soldiering, that always began with the uniform. They had coats and caps only, and boots too big for them were issued, and these at Garadon's insistence. "You're only going to grow," he told them, with a wink. "Can't have you running barefoot 'cause your toes are bursting out of your sole."

Adam and Goff's chief amusement was predicting the success of the other orphans, the young ones, in Time's platoon. One pair of green privates who joined the 6th before the Moases but after the Perryville fight in early October brought much unintended mirth to the unit, day and night.

Both men, and they claimed to be twenty, had poor eyesight. Private Rolen saw vivid color, and his eyes were the lightest of blue and sparkled in reflection and wonder, riveting a casual observer's attention. Everything he saw after an arm's length was miserably out of focus. Rolen was constantly slapping at Private Stone's shoulder in a sincere attempt at camaraderie and a selfish act of proximity, and the smaller Stone would simply absorb the good natured blasts and sometimes erupt with a punch to Rolen's chest that would send the blue-eyed soldier gasping and coughing. Private Stone saw sharp images, often describing natural or man-made objects to Rolen of those elements at a great distance, but all Stone's images were different shades of white, gray, and black.

Where Rolen would marvel at the hues in the sky, its blues and whites, and then catch the streak of a red cardinal against the deep green and brown of the forest, Stone would shrug. Where Stone would say the merchant Mother Corn had extra blankets and fresh milk in jugs before anyone could discern the trader's goods, Rolen would accept Stone's assertion as fact, rewarding good news with a hearty slap to the back.

Rolen and Stone feigned high thought and overconfidence, and brought much laughter with their deep philosophical conversations.

Rolen stood, arms spread, after two hours of close order drill, marching left-right-left back and forth across a flat clay meadow being utilized as a parade deck by crisscrossing companies. Marching in unison is easy to a casual observer, but small units take great pride in perfection of execution to drill commands, and officers placed much value on the instant obedience that would be required in the heat of battle. Garadon had complimented the 4th platoon of Company G, and the young orphans were proud of their hard-earned recognition.

"Boys! I am ready!"

"Ready for what, Rolen?"

"I am ready for battle with the enemy!"

"After marching in a straight line?" asked Stone, biting in sarcasm.

"Yes! And so are you! So are we all!"

"No, no you're not ready for anything, and neither am I." Stone went up to Rolen and punched him in the upper chest. "Don't go wishing for it, Rolen. Besides, it's too cold to fight."

@@@

Time looked at the clouds above and envied them. Their constant movement, sometimes thick, sometimes muscular, often stacked high, and then thin and veiled. Storms were created when clouds conflicted, dark and complicated one moment, invisible another. Clouds went where and when they took themselves, accountable to nature, covering the mood of the day, often entertaining, but always looked up to for a glimpse of the majesty of life.

Billy interrupted Time's reverie. "Where does the wind go, Sergeant Time?"

Time was annoyed, enjoying the one moment of solitude he had had in several days. A child's question, this boy soldier should have parents to answer him, but they were long gone. Billy clutched his utensils at his side in his left hand, a cup of hot water in his right. Time had no idea where wind went, but knew that Billy needed some kind of reassurance. “Private, the wind keeps going, unless it gets too tired. Then it just stops.”

Billy accepted the answer immediately as a truth of nature. His sergeant had spoken.

“Sergeant, do the Yankees care about their dead like we do?”

“Yes. Yes, of course, private.”

Billy was unmoved, and furrowed his brow. “I feel sorry for them, in a way, Sergeant Time. They’re so far from home.”

“Do not feel sorry for them, not ever. They feel none for themselves. They certainly feel none for you.”

@@@

Garadon was lecturing the boys, requiring them to stand at attention because of a trifling error during the afternoon drill.

“If your weapon jams, try to clear it. Those of you with Enfield’s should have a good time of it. You muzzle loaders gotta keep your powder dry. We move on line, frontal assault for the most part, but your eyes and your ears will keep you alive. Not your head. The enemy fears this to a certain degree, but that means casualties are higher. You must keep moving. Your weapon jams, pick up the weapon from the fallen next to you if you can’t clear your rifle.”

Goff, even though at attention, always struggled with impulse control, and spoke without thinking, “Why do we do a front assault? Is there a better way?”

Garadon was at first furious with the break in protocol, but he remembered Time’s rule: Teach first, discipline later.

"That's a good question, Private Moas," and in a louder parade deck voice, "Parade Rest," putting the platoon at a modified at-ease.

"The frontal assault is easier for officers to control, especially," here Garadon could not resist rolling his eyes, "political appointees. But flanking maneuvers, from the side, or rear envelopment, from the enemy's rear, work fine. The Indians are best at this. I have a lot of respect for Indians, especially in war."

Rolen spoke, boldly, "But we're smaller targets! We're perfect for a frontal assault!"

Stone shook his head. "Fool."

Rolen slapped Stone's shoulder with gusto. "And some are smaller than others, ha!"

Stone drove the flat butt stock of his parade rest rifle down onto Rolen's boot toe. The private howled, and as the platoon laughed Garadon realized it would be a small miracle if any of these boys survived the winter.

Fish was insistent, seeing nothing funny with the antics of Rolen and Stone.

"But why a frontal assault? Just for officers to see us die quicker?" Fish despaired.

Billy picked up the intention. "We should be hit and run and shoot and run, again and again."

"Yes. Yes, we should. But we won't." Sergeant Time had walked up behind his platoon, after having observed its drill work from a distance. He had reached the same silent conclusion as Garadon, only long, long before.

The orphans turned toward the commanding voice as one.

"We should stay in a defensive posture, I believe. The Union would have to come to us, on our terms. Our current strategy lacks a certain," and Time scratched his trimmed beard, "uh, plan for a final result. I believe our leadership thinks the Yankees will just quit."

"They will! We'll kill 'em if they don't!" Even Adam was caught up in the moment.

Time sighed. "I don't think they'll ever quit, not with Lincoln as president. Listen carefully. They are here. At the gate of your home. We cannot ignore them. We cannot hide. We have no recourse. It will be all or nothing."

Garadon murmured to himself, expecting the tension of the moment to mask his words but they carried to each boy soldier in the platoon. "Then we'll have nothing."

@@@

Central Tennessee's bright sun and gentle hills and temperate climate most of the year poorly hid the essential conflict of boiling militia straining to acquire land. More importantly, to keep it. The farmland was fertile, and had made many estates wealthy from its production for generations. The armies of both the North and the South knew that whichever force held Nashville, and then south to Chattanooga, would be guaranteed to be well-fed.

The axis from Nashville to Chattanooga to Atlanta would also control rail movement, crucial to the North, existential to the South. Both armies knew this, too.

Between an abundant food supply and rapid transportation, the axis may prove to be pivotal in determining the outcome of the war, many believed.

November turned to December and each day grew colder. The army of the South drilled and dug, drilled and cleaned weapons, drilled and did everything it could to stem the growing bitter cold.

The orphans grappled with the gravity of their own lives interrupted. To be part of the Orphan Brigade was a mixed honor, but to be a real orphan in the brigade was a unique macabre distinction. The boys wore it like a badge. Nearly all embraced the soldierly life as if in a religious trance, eager to perfect the rote ministrations of instant obedience to commands, the application of effective fire discipline, and the ultimate manifestation of manhood: the courage of martial combat.

Just boys, an orphan platoon of an orphan company of an orphan brigade, Time's own. Time lectured and demonstrated constantly, with Garadon a capable and credible foil who would yield to the initial walk-through exercise, then resist with increasing power as the technique of the rifle thrust, or bayonet fighting, or effective hand to hand and escape was observed with rapt attention.

"If all else fails, your fists may be effective, but you are better off with a rock or a sturdy switch," Time intoned.

"You will never throw your knife, but throw a rock if you can," deadpanned Garadon.

The boys of the orphan platoon murmured with seriousness of purpose.

"You rascals wrestle and fight amongst each other all the time. You have your whole lives to do that. The difference now is that if you do not prevail," and Time hesitated, looking directly at the Moas brothers, "if you do not win with finality, the soldier, the enemy, will kill you outright. No hesitation."

Garadon looked off, above Time's head, as two hawks dove into the trees many a yard distant. He had missed his cue from Time to elaborate.

"Corporal Garadon. Corporal, you're not thinking of that girl again, are you?" Time's repeated use of the subordinate's rank was meant to chastise, and it was effective.

"No, no, Sergeant Time." He was now alert. "Winning with finality. Sometimes winning is just getting away and back to safe lines."

Goff jumped up. "You mean, run away?"

"Yes." Garadon stared a hole into the dirt at Goff's feet.

"Yes, private, yes. Back to our lines. Remember there is always one soldier worse off than you are. Find him," Time wanted to fill in Garadon's imaginary hole with loose dirt, "or find our lines."

Garadon was experienced, and wanted to lay out the expectation with gravity. "Private Moas. Once you've made your assault, assuming you're not wounded, and that you've lost your weapon and your knife, and are fighting with rocks and sticks... yes. Run away."

Time would not challenge the statement. The boys nodded in understanding mixed with the shock of the reality they found themselves in.

They repeated dry fire exercises from standing and prone positions, some punching cartridges or mimicking paper, ball, flint and front loading. A few had weapons that could load more than two rounds. Live fire in December was not allowed. Beyond their own normal garrison noises of a workday filled with drill, the colder afternoon air of the approaching winter carried the sound of other camps.

Northern camps.

In guarded moments, Time and Garadon would trade rumors and speculate on what was a bleak future. Between the cold and a nearly constant misty and unrelenting rain, and then the louder and louder rumble of unmistakably growing Union troops, the worm of doubt crept into the imagination of both experienced men.

"With Nashville fallen, the road and rail to Chattanooga has to be kept closed to the Union until after winter. By then we'll be reinforced with..."

Time cut off Garadon. "And the Union will be reinforced, too. Probably with more cannon. Certainly with more men."

@@@

The boy soldiers seldom sat as a group at night. Their youth implied low rank, and thankless chores and working parties of the worst sort were their lot.

Two weeks before Christmas rumors were running through the camp that Nashville was controlled by the Union. A winter campaign was inevitable.

"Move a little, will ya? I can sit here, too." Goff Moas said to his brother, Adam.

"Alright, quit gripin'."

The boy Fish was talking to himself. "I am ready, I truly am."

"No, you're not, Fish," said Billy, his voice rising, "And neither am I!"

"You'll be ready when the time comes." Corporal Garadon had just entered the lighted area of the fire, leaning on his Enfield even though the platoon knew Sergeant Time told everyone else to stop doing so.

Goff, Adam, Fish and Billy all looked up in unison, Fish grinning wildly. Rolen and Stone pretended being uninterested.

"I am ready, Garadon, I am!"

"Corporal Garadon, private. You may be ready but that doesn't mean you get to be stupid."

The boys all laughed at that, and Goff threw a stick at Fish, missing his head by a full yard.

"Hey, don't throw your knife!" Adam said, and everyone nodded and chuckled.

Goff took his cue. Puffing up his chest, jutting his jaw, and squinting with one eye, Goff looked down his nose and spoke in deliberately gravelly tones.

"Never throw you knife. You've just thrown away your last weapon. You won't hit squat. You'll just anger your enemy and he'll," Goff paused to spit and take an exaggerated deep breath, "just kill you with it." Emphasizing the last few words, embellishing the tone and inflection, and he had just barely finished when he had all the boys laughing, Garadon, too, and a few stragglers who were drawn to the animated conversation that resembled fun.

"And. I. Mean. Never." Goff finished, and the tone was perfect, the mimicry of Time's mannerisms quite good, and the laughter was louder than ever.

"Well, at least you listened, Private Moas."

Time had stepped out of the shadows, directly behind Goff, and he placed a hand on the frozen private's shoulder. The others had already covered their own faces in shock and fear and hysterics.

Garadon kept chuckling. "Yep. A lesson well-learned, Sergeant Time."

"Men," said Time. They all looked up, engaged, alert, for they were always spoken to as boys, and even referred to each other in those terms.

"You will need to remember your training. Jokes are fine, as long as the lesson takes hold." He smiled. "I hope that's not your only imitation, Goff."

"Oh, no, Sergeant Time, he has lots of 'em. Lots!" Spat Fish, who loved the nightly shows.

Everyone threw a stick or imaginary stone his way. Goff slumped in exasperation.

"I feel sorry for the northerners. I do. There's more of us. This is our land, they just don't know it," said Adam.

Time pressed Goff's shoulder to sit down.

"Do not feel sorry for them, Adam Moas. Again, they feel none for you, or for themselves."

@@@

On Christmas Eve, the cold bit into the folds of tents and coats, and rations were cut back in anticipation of the winter campaign. Fires were permitted, although the strains of Union pipe and drum could be heard echoing around the night sky north of Murfreesboro. The word was that there would be no fight before Christmas, and both armies attempted to enjoy the benefits of knowing there were at least two more sunrises in each of their futures.

The soldiers of the 6th Kentucky reveled in their position cloaked by heavy woods, and fires were built, large and smoky, with no concern for the Union position, as even a bad general would discern that an army will move a bivouac set up for Christmas. They believed themselves ready.

Boredom becomes the greatest enemy. A soldier can accept no pay, no mail, cold food and a wet bedroll, but the absence of information of the war and their part in it could have devastating consequences. The ugliness of rumor was exceeded only by the Medusa of no word at all. Into this breach of nothingness and speculation the truth sometimes walks in, plain as day. And just as plain is the stringent argument, and the perceived knowledge of the intense soldier, who, even if wrong, will win the moment.

The boys of 4th platoon, Company G, had finished their evening meal, and were alternating chewing tobacco, smoking it, sipping hot and weak coffee, and listening to the sounds of the night. A private from another unit who the boys did not recognize came into their campfire light, visibly cold, but face flushed from exertion. He had been running.

"Did you hear about the corporal in Company E?"

Adam spoke first. "Asa Lewis, yes. He deserted."

The runner was adamant. "No, he did not! His enlistment was up!"

Billy said, "But you can't just get up and go."

Fish offered, "But his mother was starving. He went to bring her money!"

"I would do the same, if my mother was alive." Goff poked the fire, sending a plume of gray and white and dirty smoke skyward.

"Well," said the runner, "Not mattering much. They're gonna hang him."

"Nah, firing squad." Billy stated, absently.

"Oh, you don't know nothin'. They won't execute him. Lewis was a hero at Shiloh," suggested Adam.

The runner was getting excited. "Yes! But they're still gonna hang him!"

"No!"

"Yes! He's not yet twenty years. Bragg wants to set an example."

"No!"

"Yes! The day after Christmas!"

"No!"

And they spoke no more of it that night, but knew that if they gave into their fears, Bragg's military justice would descend upon them. To a man, they despised the commanding general.

Asa Lewis was executed by firing squad on December 26th, for being absent without permission to visit his ailing mother, even though his enlistment had legally ended. This solidified Bragg's legacy as one of an abuse of leadership.

@@@

Part Two

The Battle of Stones River

...eternal life to those who seek glory, honor, and immortality through perseverance in good works, but wrath and fury to those who selfishly disobey the truth and obey wickedness.

Romans 2:5-11

5

Before the Battle

It was December 28th and nightfall was a few short hours away.

Wayne's Hill was a promontory to the east of Stones River that afforded a perfect view of the open farmland to the west of the crooked river. The hill was steep to its west, and the gradual slope to its south was ideal for effective troop placement with some measure of concealment. It was also an easy route for cannon movement and position. At its widest point, north to south, it ran half a mile with its peak at dead center. North of Murfreesboro, Wayne's Hill was the highest location except for the mile within the town limits, much of this area reserved for General Bragg's headquarters company. North of Bragg was the Orphan's Brigade under Major General Breckinridge's command. Brigadier General Hanson commanded the extreme left flank east of the river, with artillery guns in direct support. It was an imposing and useful position. Pickets were formed at the southern base of Wayne's Hill.

Hanson had four Kentucky regiments at this extreme left position east of the river. The 2nd, 4th, 6th, and 9th, along with the 41st Alabama, which was not much more organized than the Kentucky irregulars. The 6th was under Colonel Lewis. Orphans, all.

Time and Garadon moved quickly and silently to the top of Wayne's Hill, and saw... nothing. Time's precious dual spy-glass could pick out nothing. They stomped back to Hanson's lines, situated by a river ford ideal for crossings or situating a headquarters company.

"I'll make my way to Hanson and try to suggest to his adjutant that we put ourselves on that hill. It makes no sense to put pickets in this saddle," Time gestured at the low swell at the base of Wayne's Hill, "and not take advantage of firing downhill. We can't fire up."

"You're right. I'll assemble the boys and harden their hearts. It may break the cold."

"Garadon."

"Yeah."

"They're soldiers. Stop calling them boys."

"But, sergeant..."

"Stop it, Garadon. They have to pull deep from somewhere, and they can't if they think they're just boys."

"Fine. And it's Corporal Garadon, you ugly cuss." Garadon's trademark grin kept the disrespect amusing.

Time smiled, shook his head, and left the corporal to his job and his own devices.

And Garadon wasted no time. "You, you, and you... what in the hell are you doing?"

The Moas brothers, Fish, Billy and a few others had lashed a carpet of moss to a tree and were hitting it with sticks.

Adam Moas answered first, the closest boy to him. "We're practicing using sticks and switches as weapons, corporal!"

Garadon shook his head, and said "stop" once, with a finality that dampened any enthusiasm.

Most of the boys simply dropped their sticks, looked down, and shuffled their boots. Only Goff looked ready to hit the moss-lashed tree again for good measure.

A familiar laugh began, low, and picked up in tempo. It was phlegmy and rough, and deep by any man's standards. Mother Corn, the itinerant merchant, was smoking a cheap concoction of bark and tobacco, sitting on one of two grips on his wagon of goods. Mother Corn was squat, broad, and well-fed. He sold all manner of sundries, approved and unapproved, to Confederate soldiers. He had an unspoken and invisible license to be anywhere at any time, and was conspicuously absent when the firing started. Rumored to be well-armed, he was fair in his trades and outright generous to the young orphans. He appeared to be a keen observer, talking to anyone who would engage him, most notably to himself. The demonstrated fact that he pulled his wagon unassisted by beast attested to the respect he was given by most men. His servile posture, slow gait, and self-professed illiteracy did not hide a palpable self-confidence. He could be mocked, but he would not be challenged. Mother Corn observed everything and commented on none of it unless asked.

But he laughed when he saw fit, and the pending explosion from Garadon was as good a time as any.

"That's enough out of you, Mother Corn. You shouldn't be this far away from the command post, anyway." Garadon did not trust Mother Corn.

"Yes, yes, corporal, you are right, of course." With that the trader shrugged, gripped his hand cart, and pushed it. When his supplies and sundries were depleted he pushed; when heavy he pulled. Soldiers eager for normal contact in their lives were flattered by the merchant's observation of personal habits, likes and dislikes.

"I'll be finding some more sack-cloth, boys, and I'll be back rightly soon. Good-bye, orphans," he sang merrily, knowing the extra cloth would be welcomed as much as a large fire on a cold night.

@@@

Later on the evening of the 28th, Time and Garadon walked among the young charges, firm in their encouragement, trying not to let their own teeth chatter. The cold bit hard. Fires were dotted through their position, with the 6th Kentucky embedded flush to the east of Stones River, three regiments to its right, which stretched for two miles. Due west, across the river, three more regiments faced west, their backs to the main road, Wilkinson Pike, and the business junction of the Nashville Pike and the Nashville & Chattanooga Railroad. The simplest private in the confederacy knew this juncture must be held at all costs.

The town of Murfreesboro was two miles to their rear, broken only by Bragg's headquarters with three regiments, and fully eight regiments in reserve in the town proper. With intelligence sporadic, the defensive position was prudent, but if not in the attack men grow weak in the cold. The fight was coming, but when?

December 29–30

There was no relief of sunlight on the morning of the 29th. The plan was clear for the Confederate forces: keep building and reinforcing breastworks, as the defense of Murfreesboro was the only clear choice for the tens of thousands of southern soldiers. The fires of both armies had cracked mightily and had risen high throughout the previous night, but after morning ablutions and coffee and one hot meal, the fires were extinguished.

Mother Corn was nowhere to be found.

The battle was imminent.

The 6th's proximity to Hanson's command post improved morale. Every orphan, especially Time's young platoon, was steely-eyed and acted with deliberation, reinforcing fighting positions, cleaning and re-cleaning weapons, or just rubbing feet to stay warm. Hanson rode through the ranks at mid-day, followed minutes later by the great Breckinridge himself.

"Good afternoon, sir." Time nodded respectfully, as the word to not salute general officers in the field was loosely followed, so as not to draw undue attention. The fact that any officer riding a horse provided an excellent sniper target was lost on the command.

"Good afternoon, sergeant. Are the men well fed?" It was routine for high ranking officers to ask enlisted men about creature comforts, only. The expectation of courage and ruthlessness in battle was presumed.

"Yes, sir, you could say over-fed. They are ready for a fight." Time nodded, as the general's horse tried to nuzzle him. This, too, was expected. The general does want to know if his men are prepared to fight and kill and win.

Recognition glimmered in Breckinridge's eyes. "You're Sergeant Time, aren't you?" The men were about the same age.

"Yes, sir."

"Watch over my young orphans, sergeant. Keep them..." and the general would not finish, pretended the horse was fussing, and cantered off.

Time watched Breckinridge speak encouragement and pump his fist to the youngsters digging and reinforcing their breastworks and firing positions down the line. He's a good officer and a fine leader, Time thought, but he's a sentimental sort and there is nothing to be whimsical about today. Or likely tomorrow.

"Sergeant Time."

"Yes, Fish, yes."

"Why are we digging and digging and then building up the same positions? Why not just go get 'em?" Fish eyed Time with the expectation of a lecture.

Time placed his hand on the boy's shoulder, and marveled in an instant how small and frail this soldier was. "Every rock you place will stop a bullet."

"*May* stop it, Fish," Garadon interrupted. "But it won't stop your nonsense. Get to the job."

A regimental runner, one of Colonel Lewis's men of the 6th Kentucky headquarters company, came to Time at a sprint. He was not much older than Fish, still a teen.

"Sergeant Time, the colonel is moving north, due north, to occupy Wayne's Hill. He needs you on line with his unit, in support of his forward, uh," he was breathing heavily and lost in thought.

"Defensive position. What else?"

"A battery, Cobb's, will follow."

"It'll be dark in an hour. Why now?"

"The colonel said too many echoes, too loud." The runner's breath relaxed quickly.

Time nodded once. It made sense. Create a barrier and do not cede the high ground a half mile away.

"Just the 6th and Cobb's battery?"

"Yes. No. The 9th, too, sergeant, sir." The soldier was wide-eyed and acutely tired.

"Do not 'sir' me. I don't remember your name, private. Are you the new runner?"

"Knox, sergeant. No, I'm sorta un-oh-ficial."

The boy was lost, Time thought, not physically, but lost from any care or leadership. He wanted to find a purpose and was probably tired of crap details.

Knox interrupted Time's reverie. "I wanted you to know as soon as I heard it. They'll be moving without delay, and you always get the word last, from what I heard." The boy risked much. He was not an official runner, but either his own initiative or another soldier or officer had thought Time, and his small platoon of orphans, real orphans, would need more time to prepare.

"Thank you, Knox. Stay close to your post, I don't want you getting mistaken for a deserter." As soon as Time stated this he regretted it. The image of Asa Lewis' execution was still raw. The irony that the private shared a last name with a commanding officer was lost on no one.

"Won't happen, sergeant, sir." With that Knox ran back to his unit.

Time briefed Garadon on the impending move, then walked off to find his direct commander. He prayed silently that they would all move out quickly in order to take advantage of both the light and the breastworks already made earlier on Wayne's Hill.

@@@

The rapid march to Wayne's Hill was welcomed for the heat generated by getting there on foot. The 6th and 9th assumed positions previously made, all in a silent pantomime of robust activity. All were on alert, specifically to a rumbling and echoing from the north, to a ford on this eastern side of Stones River. The 6th was on the left flank of the hill, and Time's unit had the extreme left position.

With his orphans dug in, Time motioned for Garadon to follow him to the highest point of Wayne's Hill, the apex well hidden by trees. He stopped, leaned against a large pine, and focused his binoculars on the ford a quarter mile below.

"That's an excellent spot for a river crossing," whispered Garadon. "I'm glad someone's here; just wish it weren't us."

Time tried focusing on the other side of the river. The ground seems to undulate there. He thought of the Union officer he had stolen the binoculars from months earlier. The officer was dying, alone, while the battle for Perryville raged around them both. Taking the spyglasses was an easy decision.

"He didn't need them anymore."

"What? Sergeant Time?"

"Never mind. Take a look. It's the dark coming or it's my eyes, I'm just not sure. Is the ground on the opposite river bank moving?"

Garadon quickly grabbed, focused, and spied the bank. "That's men, Union men. Stomping their feet. Bending up and down to stay warm. Hundreds of 'em."

"Go find the colonel. If they move across I'll shout. Send the skinny Moas boy here."

The sun set in an instant.

Time tried to see what Garadon saw, could not, but knew what was imminent. The Yankees were about to take the hill, likely being under the assumption it was unoccupied.

"Yes, sergeant!" Adam Moas was alert and serious.

"Start going to all the fighting positions. Tell everyone to hold their fire until I give the command."

"Yes, sergeant!" and Moas was gone.

He's a good lad and a damn fine soldier, thought Time. I wish they all were one or the other.

Garadon was back.

"The colonel wants us off this hill and back to the low fighting positions. Let the pickets do their job. Reinforcements from Hanson's brigade will take 'em before they can muster on the Hill."

"Let's do it, then. Not on line, but in file. Hurry."

In less than an hour the Union forces were crossing Stones River and scattered the Confederate pickets. By now Colonels Lewis and Hunt had their regiments prepared to deploy to re-take Wayne's Hill.

The order to move went out, again and again. The darkness was in the favor of the Rebels. They had been over this ground before, though even in familiar territory the absence of light will change the range, contour and slope of the smallest of ground.

"I can hear them," whispered Fish.

"You won't hear much very soon," said Goff.

The familiar whine and crash and boom of artillery to their rear masked the 6th's movements. It calmed and panicked at the same moment. Glad for its support but fearful of the stray shell, the young soldiers knew there would be inevitable infantry contact, and their anxiety was making the air hot and the skin cold.

"I can't see," said Billy.

"Stay with me," said Adam.

A few hundred yards to the front and the movement on the hill changed and subsided.

"Get on that hill and stay there!"

The fresh command was a relief. Expecting and dreading a fight but not wishing to delay it, the 6th moved quickly, covering the last quarter mile to the top of Wayne's hill in a few short minutes.

The Yankees were gone. If Time or Garadon could have seen the river below, they would have witnessed the Union forces in retreat, moving quickly back over the river, away from the Rebels. The 6th never fired a round, as the pickets and the 9th and other elements of the command made quick work of the surprised Union troops.

In an hour Colonel Hunt was back in control of Wayne's Hill.

Rumors swirled quickly after battles. The losses and the victories, large and small, were shared, embellished, and boasted upon. Heroism and cowardice were reviewed and reviled step by painful step.

The non-battle of Wayne's Hill was no different.

@@@

By mid-day of the 30th it was evident the battle would be fought miles away from Wayne's Hill, on the far west flank of the entire Rebel field position. The previous night, after holding Wayne's Hill, the 6th and 9th were ordered back to the Murfree House, less than a mile south of the Hill, closer to the command posts of both Breckinridge and Bragg; by that evening the 2nd and 4th Kentucky were fully dug in on Wayne's Hill. The rumors of no fighting were damnable, as the imagination bred from inactivity was never a friend to the soldier.

Time was relieved. Garadon was anguished. They could hear the rough confused echo of battle all day long. Today's fighting, with Breckinridge's division now in reserve, began to gnaw at Time as the day wore on, and his anxiety, though well-hidden, would not escape the harsh glare of admiring youth.

"Are we in for it, Sergeant Time?"

"What? No. The battle is to the west, and south, on the other side of the river." Time had to pause as the cacophony of artillery and volleys of rifle fire were increasing in intensity. "We'll sit this one out, I think."

Garadon, always faithful when needed, said gently to the gaggle of boy soldiers. "The fight will come soon enough, lads. You're trained. You're fed and equipped. And right now you're dry. Don't think too much on this. Be ready. Just be ready."

A familiar low tonal laugh interrupted.

"Yes, boys, be ready."

It was Mother Corn, again.

"I don't want you about here, merchant," spat Garadon, "and I don't want you agreein' with anything I say." The corporal unconsciously wiped his hands on the front of his trousers.

"Okay, I'll go, corporal, I'll go. I think these boys appreciate your knowledge of the soldier's art," he said, then hacked at a wet cough, and began to pull his cart toward the river, for what appeared to be an easier walk to the Murfree House, and Bragg's headquarters.

Time, Garadon, and the orphans watched the squat trader amble away, his cart heavy.

"He speaks well for an illiterate man," said Time.

"And how in hell does he get so many fresh supplies? There's a fight here!" Garadon was becoming angry just thinking about the possibilities. "Maybe he's stealing, or making one-sided bargains, or..."

"Let it go, corporal. We'll keep an eye on our charges. We can't solve all the problems around here, and others will have to keep an eye on their own. I don't like the bum, either. Doesn't mean he can't make a living."

Garadon nodded repeatedly, willing himself to take Time's instruction and advice, in spite of his own substantial misgivings.

The noise of battle would not end until dark on the 30th, and then only lessened by artillery fire.

@@@

Dawn December 31st

That morning the little things became big. Time knew that the largest tasks of men and nations are small when measured against the most base of human conditions. The South may lose the battle and the war today, but right now he had to relieve himself before his mortality could even be considered. Then he needed to get busy, and soon.

"Get up get moving, we're goin' back to Wayne's Hill."

Sergeant Time and Corporal Garadon were kicking their unit now sandwiched within the 6th Kentucky. They had just received orders from the unofficial runner, Private Knox, a half-breed some said, but Garadon got the word was he was a solid soldier fearless of gunfire if not outright ruthless at heart. Both would accept Knox, but they harbored a lingering doubt as to his loyalties beyond the orphans.

Time kept his orphan platoon low by the river, as he could sense the Confederate pickets to the west of it. Garadon did the precision work of placing the boy soldiers at the base of the hill, facing due west. The 6th Kentucky's mission was to keep the Union from crossing the water at this juncture.

The artillery barrage began after 0700. The gunfire from the top of Wayne's Hill kept the Union at bay that morning. Time and Garadon nodded back and forth to each other while encouraging the orphans to sit tight. They knew the 6th was at a deep bend in the Stones River, and that would keep them out of the fight, for now. Time's platoon faced an almost sheer embankment straight up from the riverbed on the opposite side of the river. There was no chance of a direct attack.

The runner, Knox, had plenty of useful information for Time. He reported that Yankee patrols had begun to probe east of the river, about a mile or two north of Wayne's Hill, at a point called McFadden's Ford.

"How big a force?"

"Brigade size, four thousand strong, they think. But the Yanks aren't using them big guns yet. Sending out only small patrols."

"Why?"

"How do I know?" Knox liked the attention, but he was not as deep a well as presumed by Time.

Time was anxious. Garadon came up hard.

"Do you think most of it is west of us?"

"No, south more like, west some, but the Yankees are on the run." Knox nodded with enthusiasm as he spoke.

Time was not impressed. "Too early in the day to take bets on a winner."

The next hour moved like a year. At 0900, Garadon had grown restless, and the young soldiers thought they saw Union pickets on the other side of the river, implausibly, and they began to become more agitated than indirect action warranted.

"Sergeant Time, can I take a look-see from the top of the Hill?"

Time handed the field glasses to Garadon. "Take someone with you."

"Fish! Private Fish! Front and center!" The boy was there in a flash, a skinny little kid holding a large rifle at port arms, absurd and emotional to see amid the chaos all around them. Garadon tugged at Fish's coat front, and nodded approval.

"Follow me."

When they reached the top of Wayne's Hill, Garadon checked in with a sergeant of the 9th, at the apex and behind a substantial Rebel battery. The sound was deafening, as repeated concussions of supporting fire were launched again and again and again.

"I need to see what's what. I have my own field glasses."

The sergeant of the 9th was older, old enough to be Garadon's grandfather. "Use my glasses, they's in better shape. We're whuppin' 'em." He placed his hands on Garadon's shoulders from the back, and pointed the corporal in the right direction. Fish stayed at port arms, a full head shorter than both men.

Garadon was amazed at the clear field of vision, but was transfixed by what he saw. West and south of Wayne's Hill, across the river, a couple miles away now brought closer, blue coats were running north in retreat, across Wilkinson Pike, in what looked like a rout. The gray had the advantage and was seizing it with a bloodlust, in full pursuit of the retreating Union forces, whose centerline was hopelessly fractured. Low Rebel guns on the field coughed fire and smoke, and in an instant a courageous non-retreating Yankee platoon fell back as one like mown grass.

Garadon pulled the glasses away from his head. He had been in battles before, and seen men fall one by one beside him, and had even taken a bullet in his hip at Perryville. But he had never seen an entire platoon killed in one flash. "It could have been any of us," he murmured, knowing that the steady artillery fire would drown out his spoken thought.

The old soldier kept his hands on Garadon's shoulders, sensing the junior man's distress. He looked at Fish, still at port arms. "You want to look?"

"No. Thank you. No." Fish could see Garadon's stricken face, and wanted no part in it.

The skies opened up with a cold, hard rain. Garadon saw his opportunity and used it.

"We'll get back. Thank you, sergeant."

"We'll see you on the other side, young fella."

@@@

Back at the low river position, Time was impatient. "What did you see, Garadon?"

"Cold, frozen men walking into certain death." Garadon was wooden and wet, with a dull stare that was more distracted than anxious.

Time was now annoyed, and grabbed the corporal's collar. "Snap to, man. What is going on?" Garadon was immediately alert, and not a little piqued.

"Look, James Time, I've walked through fire with you. I've carried the wounded and buried the dead, and sometimes just their parts. But I have never seen a whole platoon, maybe two dozen men, flattened to death in one blast of a cannon. Never."

Fish remained at port arms, his mouth a perfect oval and his eyes wide and unblinking. To see death was one thing, he thought. Yet to see the only two men committed to keeping him and the others alive, arguing with each other, was terrifying.

"And they were facing us. The rest of that company or regiment or whatever just turned tail and ran. Those soldiers looked right at death, and never knew what happened." Garadon looked back up the Hill.

Time had to see for himself. "It's about 10 now. Keep a hard eye here. Billy!" The boy, soaked, came at a sprint. "Come with me." They ran up the hill, using due care with the sludge up the slope building from the persistent rain.

@@@

Time came up to the same elderly sergeant.

"Been expecting you, Sergeant Time. Helluva battle below us." The constant roar of Rebel cannon firing yards away made conversation nearly impossible. The smoke clung to the earth from the rain, but sped north and east, away from Time's line of sight. "Here."

Time grabbed the field glasses, and was nudged in the general direction; he needed no further prompting.

It appeared that the Yanks were surrounded west of the river, though closer to Wayne's Hill than yesterday, with the Rebel artillery doing its worst. Clumps of men tried to hide behind a single tree, and not just one tree, but a scattered dozen of them. Boulders and rocks that could shelter two men were harboring ten, men who tried to climb into each other's coats for warmth, for protection, for life.

Rebel soldiers, freezing but maintaining a shoulder to shoulder front for miles, kept firing, kept moving forward, and kept formation, even in the face of comrades dropping dead from violent wounds. At the center of the engagement all semblance of Yankee order appeared abandoned and at several points Union artillery pieces were immediately deserted. Good guns, all.

Billy was less intimidated than Fish had been earlier. Cold rain can make a soldier very quiet or very insistent, and this boy was the latter.

"Watcha see, sergeant? Are we winning?"

"Our troops have the high ground, and we have just overrun some Yankee artillery. We'd never let that happen. Never. Never leave high ground or firepower, Billy."

"Seems like we got both right here. Just loud." Billy shouted at Time's ear.

"Yeah, we have a better spot downhill." Time didn't want to state the obvious. Sooner or later the Yankees would draw a deadly bulls-eye on the guns on Wayne's Hill and rain fire. With impunity.

"Can I look?" shouted Billy, jumping up twice.

Time began to hand Billy the binoculars, but the boy was holding the pocket satchel with the utensils in front of him, as an offering.

"Hold these, please. I want both hands on the glasses." He grabbed them and instinctively trained his sight to the field of battle, now less than a mile away.

"Sergeant Time! There! There! Rebels coming across our front! They're advancing, steady and true!"

"Give that to me," barked Time, unsure what Billy saw, mistaking enthusiasm for fear. There, west and a little south, Tennessee regulars were moving like a tidal wave of soaked frozen demons straight into the Union force, using Nashville Pike as a guide right into the heart of the Union line. He was proud and anxious. The battle is turning away from us, he thought, but it isn't noon and the Yanks haven't given ground so quickly, ever.

He dropped the utensil pocket, which Billy caught effortlessly as if in anticipation, before the pouch could hit the ground.

A roar of full throated cheer went up and carried to Wayne's Hill, from farther west. A pincer maneuver by Rebels at the farthest and most westward reaches of the battle had begun and been repulsed, and, there – Yankee reinforcements on line. And they pressed hard. The Rebel advantage was less than a quarter mile away, while the Union was advancing back over lost ground a mile or so further west.

Still it rained.

Both sides taking terrible losses, but the men who kept moving, kept advancing, appeared to prevail. To stay still meant to die. To succumb to the creature comfort of futilely trying to stay dry was a precursor to death.

"Let's go, Billy. We have work to do."

Time handed the sergeant the glasses, and their eyes met. The elder gripped Time's forearm.

"Watch the boys. I'll pray for ya."

Time and Billy ran and slid down the hill.

@@@

Adam and Goff were standing behind the trees, watching the battle enter their vision piecemeal. The west embankment was above them, but the concussion from the field beyond their line of sight was unmistakable.

An enterprising private from another platoon had climbed a nearby pine unaffected by the artillery fire. He reported sporadically when begged to do so, in a torrent of shouted words.

"The Yankee pickets to our front have been pushed back by our regulars. I think Tennessee. Wait! One of our companies is retreating! Our boys are taking a helluva beating with musket and big gun fire. Get out! Get out of them trenches! Oh! Oh! We're setting fire to a house, which looks gutted! Huzzah! Wait! Wait! The dang rain put the fire out! All that work wasted." It was lost on the soldier that it was the building of the house that was wasted, not the attempted fire to destroy it.

The rain continued off and on, moving in off-white waves across the rows of men fighting and falling, cursing and screaming, walking forward into the face of glory or oblivion. The strains of concussion and explosion mingled in a macabre concordance with cries of pain and frustration, peppered with the occasional and predictable, "God help me!"

"Our boys are walking on our own dead! We're losing ground!"

The runner Knox came up to Time. Time spoke first. "Why aren't we supporting the attack? There're four or five regiments on this hill. Don't need all of 'em to protect the guns!"

Garadon was equally concerned. "Are we losing ground along that pike?"

Knox cut them off. "There was a lot of hollering at the command an hour ago, around noon. But you're staying put for the time being."

Garadon went back to the treed reporter of events, the best source of intelligence he could use. Time returned to his entrenched position, sitting on a rock under a large pine in an attempt to stay dry.

"Hey, there, sergeant. Some tobacco?"

Mother Corn stood above him, his face and the front of his tunic dry. He smiled. In his hand he offered a pouch of pipe tobacco.

"I don't smoke a pipe. Got anything rolled?" Time avoided looking directly at the merchant.

Mother Corn beamed. "Sure do." He reached into a fold and produced a thick cigarette, cupped under his hand. Time grabbed it, and just as quickly the trader lit it. Time pulled deeply, dragging the worst of the smoke into his lungs when it should have lingered in his mouth. He held it, and closed his eyes. Exhaling slowly, he would not cough, the cold and rain suppressing everything except the sheer pleasure of the burn in his lungs and the dizziness in his head. He was alive. The selfish pain and pleasure of the fresh rolled cigarette was more than comforting. It was magnificent.

Mother Corn read his mind. "As good as a woman?"

Time shook his head, the blue white smoke finishing out his nose. "No, no. Not even close."

The reporter up the tree screamed, "Good Lord! There's one of our boys holding his own arm like a sword! He's waving it at the Yanks! Agggh! He struck one with it! He's beatin' him with it!"

Garadon started to shout something, but his own curiosity about the battle was too acute. He looked at Time, who was finishing his smoke, not thirty feet away.

"I guess it's better we know what's going on, than not knowing, right, Time?"

"Sergeant Time, Garadon. Go check your lines. If they haven't rested, tell 'em to. And make sure they've eaten. No fires." Time now directed his heat to the treed reporter. "You! Yeah, you. You're now a lookout. If any force makes a break for the river, sound the alarm. No other report out of you is necessary! Understood?" The private nodded repeatedly.

Garadon grumbled his assent to Time and moved off slowly.

Mother Corn was still at Time's side. "I hear we've captured some Union doctors, real surgeons. Whattya think of that?"

Time gave him a dark stare. "What do you think we'll do?"

"Why, hang 'em!"

"You're an ass, Mother Corn. An unintelligent, no-good ass. You don't hang doctors. We'll trade for 'em, like civilized people. Bragg is a prick, but he's a military man, not a killer for the sake of it."

Adam and Goff were at Time's side and had witnessed the exchange. They looked at their feet, remembering Time's defense of Bragg not a few days before, when Bragg had executed the deserter, Asa Lewis.

"Well?" Time's anger at the merchant now transferred to the Moas boys.

"Got any more rolled tobacco, Mother Corn?" Goff knew how to change a subject.

The treed soldier could not contain himself, and was encouraged by his own sergeant to give him more information. Time ignored it as best he could.

"Men are running in all directions, gray and blue, some with blankets wrapped 'round 'em, running for miles! I can't tell who's winning! Some's retreatin', some's chargin', some's just runnin' right by the enemy just to get to a tree for cover!"

The 6th Kentucky could hear the battle, but without the reporter's eyes could see almost nothing from its river bed position. The private continued to report that the Yankees held the Nashville Pike just north of Wayne's Hill, and had become more organized as the battle wore on. The fighting reached a crescendo of artillery fire by 3 p.m., and Time's platoon within the 6th could feel the incessant concussion of a quarter mile away, could taste the acrid black smoke, and could smell the fear of both armies. Time and Garadon never returned up the hill that afternoon. They had seen enough for a lifetime in the few minutes they had witnessed earlier in the day.

"Praise God we can't see it," said Rolen.

@@@

It began to darken by 4 p.m., and the temperature dove down to freezing. Knox came to Time at a gallop. "We're all to go to the top of Wayne's Hill. They'll place us behind the artillery."

"When?"

"Right now."

Time called Garadon over, who still sulked over the petty rebuke from earlier. Time told him the plan as he knew it, and to get it done right away.

"Yes, sergeant." Just a bit of hesitation, but enough to communicate disapproval, but not quite disdain. Time let it pass.

@@@

Hours later, after the position for the 6th was completed on Wayne's Hill, Garadon challenged Time. "No fires?" Garadon acted incredulous.

"No, of course not. The guns are here. The Yankees will use the fires to draw a plan for their artillery, or to guess troop strength." Time knew that Garadon was perfectly aware of the reasons, but he needed the experienced corporal's support, and not an argument. "Look, if you were in my boots, you would expect me to understand that."

"It's effin' freezing, sergeant. I mean, sheesh."

Time wanted to show solidarity with Garadon. Night had come early, before 5 p.m. It was now nine, and a shot had not been heard in hours. Certainly the Yanks were solidifying their defensive positions. The rumors were that the Rebels had won the day, and had kept the railhead and the southern route of the Nashville Pike.

"I can still hear 'em, sergeant. Them Yankees haven't gone anywhere. If we beat 'em, they don't know it." Garadon was close enough so that his voice didn't carry and they could speak in confidence of not being overheard. Time knew he was right.

Time also realized he didn't know Garadon's first name. Everyone called him Garadon. It had a martial air and he responded only to it. Time thought that calling him 'corporal' would be demeaning, especially since he was the platoon sergeant, second in command, to only a sergeant. A Yankee one at that.

"Garadon."

"Yeah."

"You're the best soldier I know. My brother, the West Pointer, is the best officer. But you are the best soldier. Thought you should know."

Garadon tried not to show either surprise or approval. He was still smarting from the earlier encounter, but he knew an apology when he heard one.

"Sergeant Time."

"Just Jim, for now."

"Just Garadon, all the same." They chuckled as their teeth chattered. "Look, Jim. We're not gonna die. Don't get all womanly on me."

Time barked a genuine "HAHAHA!" and threw an imaginary stone, which Garadon pretended to duck from.

"I'll get to work, make 'em rub their feet and such. Guard's set. We're pulling more than we should for the brigade, as you can imagine." He paused and patted his own chest. "Good night, sergeant."

"Wake me at the mid-watch?"

"Done."

Time was exhausted, but knew without fire it would be difficult, probably impossible, to sleep. If he did drift off he might freeze to death. He would spend the night checking his orphan platoon, ensuring they were resting or on watch, no random attempts at fires, and were not dead from the damp cold.

Images flashed through his restless mind, some seen and others he did not witness, but were told to him and he could envisage fully.

A platoon of soldiers falling backward in an instant, limbs and heads flying, all dead. In the blink of an eye.

Men standing still in the freezing rain waiting to be bayonetted.

Men huddled behind trees, throwing the smallest and weakest into the line of fire.

Men crying for their mothers, begging to live.

Men swinging severed limbs like weapons.

Through all the images, a constant barrage of gunfire pops and artillery booms. The earth had stopped shaking long ago except his teeth chattered rhythmically, and Time kept waiting for it to start all over again.

The cold seeped into his bones, rainwater dripping from his neck down his back, the coarsened wool absorbing and chafing what little warm skin he had left. Each breath was ragged, his ribs hard and icy, the hair under his nose frozen in mucous and sweat. He sighed, allowing the soft yielding and unexpected embrace of slumber to take him away.

@@@

6

The New Year, 1863

Dawn on the first.

Knox woke Time. Garadon was missing, he said.

"What do you mean, missing?" Time was in a fog, having actually slept uninterrupted for three hours.

"Can't find him. He relieved you at 0300, right?" Goff Moas was with Time when he woke Garadon at that hour, who was instantly alert. Time and Goff shuffled off to get sleep, knowing dawn would come early. "The Moas boy says he hasn't seen him since the relief." Knox shook his head as if he knew something obvious that Time was blind to.

"He isn't missing, Knox. Maybe you don't know everything. Is the captain meeting with us this morning?" Knox appeared to be an effective runner, but he was no authority. Time commanded this young orphan platoon, and everyone knew that Breckinridge himself had a hand in it. Time was not an officer, but he was a fighter and he was responsible. Knox blanched.

"Oh, no, sergeant. He's at brigade now, meeting with Hanson himself. There's..."

"There's no plan, Sergeant Time. A perfect mess." Garadon stood above Time and Knox, on an empty crate.

Time shot a look at Knox. "Missing, huh?"

Garadon waved him off. "Knox, you can't brow-beat our men for information, even if they can't shave." To Time he said, "Goff came to me after his, uh, conversation with Knox." Back to Knox, "You idiot." Back to Time. "Bad news, sergeant. First, there's no plan. We're picking up our dead from the field after morning chow. So're the Yankees. The real problem is that we're out of ammunition west of the river. Resupply is tough in this weather, so now they want to redistribute. Hanson is fighting it. Breckinridge is backing Hanson. Bragg thinks he's won the field, but from the looks of it we're all in about the same spot before yesterday's hell-hole. Only colder." He jumped down from the crate toward Knox. "And wetter." And a long step. "And real, real angry." He stood nose to nose with Knox. In a fair fight Knox would not last five seconds. A crowd was drawing, and Knox would not likely back down, thinking that taking a beating would be better than the humiliation of backing down. Garadon might get some pleasure after the long cold wet nasty night. Time intervened from where he sat.

"Get out of here, Knox. Bring me something useful." No use asking for hot food, Time thought. Still no fires.

An hour later, the word came that cooking fires would be allowed until further notice. Garadon and Time were drinking weak but steaming hot coffee.

"It's a draw." Garadon had made his rounds, both of his orphans and as close to Brigadier General Hanson's command post as he dared. He was bursting with news.

"There are over 3,000 Union prisoners, and at least as many dead. Cavalry is reporting somewhere near 200 captured wagons, most just destroyed."

Time was cautiously impressed, but annoyed. Curious, he knew better than to interrupt Garadon, and even if he tried it was unlikely he could have slowed his corporal. The Moas brothers and several others stayed within earshot. "Cavalry is always bragging. They don't let the truth get in the way of their heroics," he said absently.

"They're arguing, sergeant. Units are mixed, confused, and not all are accounted for. There's a fearful shortage of rifle ammunition..."

"They won't take ours!" Goff was much too confident and spoke out of line.

"...and the Yankees are still on the field, still at the Pike north of what they call the round forest, and still collecting their dead."

Time was now more concerned. "They haven't retreated to Nashville? Knox said we won the day!"

Garadon spat crookedly, and stifled a sneeze. "That boy doesn't know his butt from his elbow."

There was a murmur of appreciative chuckling from the orphans. Soldiers of any size and stripe enjoy humor wrapped around creative cussing, even if it was watered down.

Time needed to confer privately with Garadon. "All right, men, back to your fighting holes. Reinforce. Build up with rock or large timber. We may be here for a while." Time thought that Wayne's Hill, Hanson's brigade position, was an ideal target for Union artillery. If they aren't leaving, Time mused, they'll start shooting again.

Time and Garadon now stood. "Sergeant, if they haven't left, it's because they can still be resupplied from Nashville. So why haven't *we* left? Bragg's whole army? From what I hear we're the only ones with ammunition. It'll take days to sort this all out."

Time pulled his old field glasses up to his face, and trained them on the stretch of land west of Stones River. Both Union and Rebel working parties were silently surveying the field, locating the wounded and the dead, and either furiously attending to the broken figures or trying to be reverent in moving the inert forms.

Rifle fire half a mile away drew his attention to a small copse of trees, tight at one point a day ago but now riddled with broken trunks and missing branches. A company of Rebels were running away from that round forest, but there was no fire from Union forces in pursuit.

"The Yankees must really want that juncture." Time saw that the copse was at a crucial point of the railroad, the Nashville Pike, and another road that ran straight north/south. I'd want to control that, too, he thought. But I wouldn't want to make too much of it today.

There was a flurry of activity on the hilltop, especially around Hanson's command tent. Someone there also saw the skirmish by the round forest to the west across the river and drew the same conclusion as Time: grab that spot, but just chase the Yankees out. No sense starting a major fight since those troops were too low on ammunition to sustain an engagement.

Time put the glasses down. "There'll be no fighting today, I suspect, Garadon. The Yankees are collecting their dead and digging. They have dozens, dozens of guns in plain sight. They're gonna put it to us, likely tomorrow."

"Or tonight." Garadon was less confident, as his vigilance had kept him alive this long. I'm sticking with my gut, he thought.

"Have the men re-do their tents, strip, and get their garments dry. We can't spend two nights with no sleep. As long as we're not detailed out, we might be fresh for tomorrow."

Garadon nodded, spittle crusting his beard from the freezing mist and sheer exhaustion. "Damn, it's cold. After I get the word out, I think I'll try to get some sleep." He walked off to his lean-to, sat, pulled off one boot, and fell back, snoring before his head hit the ground. Time smiled, and called over the Moas brothers and gave them the same orders and to get the word out right away.

Time looked back over the field with his binoculars. Parties of two and three Confederates would examine a body and place it on a litter. One pair of Rebels stopped walking with an empty stretcher and whistled loudly at a pair of Union soldiers not thirty yards distant, performing the same task. One of the Rebels pointed to the ground as the other waved to show he was unarmed. The Yankees trudged woodenly to pick up their fallen comrade, found by the Rebels. When the Union boys reached where the Rebels had pointed, one Yank fell to his knees, buried his face in his hands, and wracked hard in what looked like sobs, but could have been the anger of shouting to a deaf God.

Time put the glasses down. I can't watch this, he thought. I'll start to build too much sympathy.

Knox walked up to him. "No more fighting today, sergeant. No one's certain where the Union positions are, given tree cover up the river." Knox paused, awaiting a comment.

Time's exhaustion was profound. "What else?"

"Bragg has returned all the Union surgeons. Just returned 'em. Can't understand it. Seems he was expecting a trade, and didn't get one."

Time coughed. "It might not have been smart, and Bragg has made his mistakes, but if their doctors can send one of their boys home, it was worth it. We are all neighbors, you know."

"Oh, c'mon, sergeant, you..."

"Look, they say they want to preserve the Union, and free slaves. We want a say in how we are governed, not by some blue-blood northerner that never worked a field." Time had done all manner of such work all over the south and west for twenty years before the war. "Killing everybody means no one gets what they want. Sending those surgeons back is a grand gesture and I respect it."

"Suit yourself. Hanson wants all commanders at his tent at 1500 hours. That includes you." Knox walked off in long strides.

@@@

"So, there's still no plan?" Garadon's voice rose.

Time was patient, but knew he must convey confidence in spite of not having any. He was on the periphery of the officer briefing, and had not heard all of it. Hanson's adjutant reiterated everything that Time already knew and witnessed. When General Hanson spoke, it was with his usual vibrancy, but it lacked... information. Before a fight troops like the platitudes of heroism and vague images of glory, but front-line leaders prefer concrete plans and objectives. There were none.

"General Breckinridge was present."

That buoyed the spirits, and there was some back-slapping and good-natured "Told you!" from several of the orphans.

"He has every faith and confidence in you all. More on the morrow. Eat, rest, stay dry or at least warm. Standard watch detail."

"Fires?"

"No. Use candles in your tents. No more than that."

Garadon had his arms crossed, shaking his head. "Where's that damn merchant Mother Corn when you need him?"

@@@

Morning on the second.

Breckinridge could feel the pressure from his subordinate commanders, good military men who respected the general's position and stature but who routinely second guessed every move or lack of it.

He decided to go look at the field for himself. Without tactical information he could not form a decent defense, let alone take the initiative. He had strong picket positions on good ground, but his men east of Stones River were reporting no movement at all to the north, which was improbable.

Limited skirmishes, sporadic artillery and a swift probing party gave him the vantage point he needed to view the Yankee position, and what Breckinridge saw was alarming. Substantial Union positions were developing a mile north of Wayne's Hill on his side of the river. He surmised that if this juggernaut of up to two brigades was not held off, the potential to envelop the Confederate position was high and quite possible. Yankee cannon west of the river would be able to provide devastating support.

Breckinridge reported what he witnessed to his superior. General Bragg had already sent a message to President Jefferson Davis that Murfreesboro was secure. The information from Breckinridge was a direct threat to not just his word, but his competence.

Bragg ordered Breckinridge to move the Union forces off their current position east of the river. Breckinridge may have sensed Bragg's ego and ambition were driving the order, when the prudent move would have been a full scale retreat to solidify command, keep unit integrity, and resupply fully. Breckinridge argued against an attack, noting, correctly, that Union artillery was in plain view, massed to fire in a wide arc to ruinous effect over the entire area east of the river, and was likely enjoying an unfettered supply chain from Nashville.

Bragg held firm.

Breckinridge briefed his subordinate generals and colonels on Wayne's Hill at about 2 p.m. General Hanson, who had ached to get into the fight just two days before, was now apoplectic that the Orphan Brigade would be the tip of the arrow in an assault over open ground on a Union position being reinforced with greater strength and artillery by the minute. An abundance of ammunition, another commander stated plainly, will not make the situation any less dreadful.

Hanson was still incensed over the execution of that poor boy, Corporal Asa Lewis. He intimated to all in attendance that he should kill Bragg with his bare hands for his serial ineptitude, and at one point in the briefing he had to be physically restrained.

@@@

At 3 p.m., Knox ran up to Time.

"The 6th is on the attack! About a mile north of here, along the side of the river, we'll be joined to our right by the rest of Hanson's command, and then the Tennesseans to Hanson's right. Guns will be on the finger to our east where the pickets are now. The boys from Louisiana will be in reserve."

"Damn. Why are we in front? These orphans, heck, they're all boys!" Time was thinking only of his own small company, but he was impressed with Knox's improved reporting and presence of mind.

"You have the extreme left, sergeant. One round loaded. Fix bayonets. Gotta be on that finger in thirty minutes, and you'll need every second. The attack starts at four."

Knox stood erect, not at attention, but certainly alert and anxious. He remained at Time's side, looking north.

"No one else to run to, Knox?"

"Lay off it, sergeant. They keep telling me to get lost, just like they forget to bring you in. If it wasn't for the colonel, you might get left on this hill."

"Make yourself useful, then. Help these boys get ready. Take the rear of our march." Time nodded to the soldier, and smiled.

"Thanks. I'll do it right." Knox bolted.

Garadon assembled the twenty five orphans of Time's platoon, and Time briefed them on the impending attack. The boys were jumping on each other like puppies. After seeing and hearing the devastation of the past couple days, and another day of rest and rumor and boredom, they thought themselves ready for battle.

"Boys, no. Soldiers all! A prayer is in order. Bow your heads. Our Father, Who art in Heaven..."

After the prayer Time's rag-tag platoon of orphans of the 6th Kentucky moved to the assembly point established on a finger a third of a mile north of Wayne's Hill. They were the last unit on the left. Garadon took that extreme spot, keeping a keen eye on his orphans once they reached the assault deployment line.

It's better we do not have too much time to dwell on this, Time thought, but we, these boys, are not ready for even a fair fight with hardened troops.

"But why attack, at this point?" Garadon half-whispered to Time.

Time kicked an imaginary stone. "It's like this. We attack, we die. We surrender, we die. We do nothing, we die. So, let's attack. Gives us purpose. At least we go on our own terms."

Garadon appreciated the flawed logic, and understood to the soles of his feet the martial stir for the 6th to take matters into its own hands.

At 4 p.m. the assault began.

@@@

The 6th remained on the extreme left of the assault line, the entire complement of Breckinridge's army to its right, the Stones River to its left. Garadon stayed to the far left, and marveled at the contrast of the peaceful flow of the river and the carnage to his right.

Billy was in awe, fumbling with his cutlery and keeping his rifle on his hip, under the disapproving glare of Garadon. He shoved them back in his pocket and assumed a proper fighting stance. We're in the assault as soon as we got here on this finger, he thought. Maybe we're behind.

Adam and Goff were to Billy's right, then Fish, and the twenty or so remaining boys of Time's unit. Time now shouted from somewhere behind to Knox to try to keep tied to the next platoon on the right, even if he had to pull a soldier by his coat-sleeve if need be to stay on line and connected. No fire was taken for 200 yards.

The formation was loose and sloppy. There was much artillery raining down to their front and in the middle of the army's assault line, but the 6th was free from it. They began to race as one through the open field, the concussion of artillery spurring them on.

Goff tried to keep up, and Adam started to run forward until Time's booming roar to *"walk steady on line"* forced him to slow down. Billy kept his eyes on Garadon every second step, and glanced to ensure he was even with Adam.

Fish stumbled, and Goff pulled him up by the arm, not missing a single step. "Thanks, Goff, you saved me!"

"No, you fool, we ain't been shot at yet."

Goff thought that they might all be safer if they had just stayed low and hidden in the open field.

What was once soft grass was now hard stalks and ice puddles, and just as it appeared that the battle would open up before them, Time's unit was spun left by the inertia of the larger assault, taking it toward the river.

Garadon shouted, but it was futile to get anyone to change direction. Billy, the Moas boys, and Fish were now crowded to within yards of the river. Time cried out something above the crash of artillery to Garadon that the boys didn't comprehend.

"Away from the river, lads, we'll fall behind the rest of the company." They ran away from the river keeping Time and the rest of his platoon to their direct front, not more than twenty yards away.

The yell from the Rebels now reached a fanatical pitch, striking fear in the Union forces heard to the front and bringing courage to the Rebels in equal force. The entire Orphan Brigade began shouting as one when it was in effective standing rifle range, and the screaming grew louder and more intense. The Rebels were in an impassioned assault.

Adam Moas could sense with his own mounting curiosity and fear that all the forces to his right were being cut down. The yells became shrieks of anger and despair, the last cries of many of the 6th, even though Time's small contingent on the extreme left flank had yet to take fire.

They were all winded from excitement and the fast-step exertion staying up with Time's men to their front. Billy, Fish, the Moas brothers, and Garadon bent their backs to climb a small rise behind the main assault line, and Fish thought that the sounds were mixed differently, that the other side of the small rise was either a fight or more Rebels.

Billy dropped his weapon from shaking so much. Adam laughed and bent to help him retrieve it, just as Garadon's foot slipped attempting to kick the fool boy for dropping his rifle. Thinking Garadon had been shot, Goff and Fish flew to the corporal's side as he fell backwards.

At the crest of the low rise Time's men stopped, shouldered their weapons as one, and fired. At the same instant, most of them fell back, at least twenty of them, flat, shot, injured, crippled or dead. The Rebel yell was now only an agonized screech of shock. Some begged to die.

Time was behind the line, under the crest by only the measure of his hat. Two boys fell on top of him. He hollered in amazement, and pushed the two off him, youngsters, both. One was quickly dead from butchery, and the other, whose shock of long black hair was the butt of many jokes and the envy of all, would be very soon, his chest injury too devastating. Time had forgotten their names.

There was no sound from the crest, where the fire had come from. Time crawled the five feet and peered over. A Yankee unit, much greater in size, was tending to the dead and wounded from the Orphan's first volley. They gave 'em as good as we got, he thought, but his anger and fear and disgust was boiling. Time looked to his right as a sister platoon came over the same slight ridge at a gallop shouting and yelling and firing. Knox was at their extreme left and almost close enough to touch, yelling and cursing and jabbing the air with his bayoneted rifle with a gusto reserved only for great vengeance or madness. Knox saw Time prone and fell beside him, breathless and wild-eyed.

Time looked to his left and discovered a clear line of sight across the river to a plateau he could not observe from Wayne's Hill, which seemed like months ago, though only hours.

"That's more guns together than I've ever seen," he said aloud to himself. "Gotta be fifty, more." The Yankee artillery pieces were massed and firing directly and constantly at the Confederate attack.

Garadon's little squad of the youngest was now prone, frozen in shock. He realized that they were alive because he wanted to kick a soldier in the behind, and he fell in the attempt. Because they came to his rescue.

"Sergeant, we're here, we're ready to press forward," shouted Garadon, rising and running to Time. The boys followed dutifully, trying and failing to avoid stomping on the strewn bodies of their fellow soldiers.

Fish was crying, and Billy suppressed a sob. Adam and Goff were holding each other at the waist, as though injured, but they kept each other on their feet.

Billy looked down at the fresh corpse of a freckled youngster who helped him polish the utensils. The freckled kid never talked much, but marveled at performing simple routine functions, and tried desperately to be clean at all times. In death he would have been disappointed, as he was filthy with stale sweat, dirt and blood, and Billy heaved a gasping sigh and prayed the boy's end had been swift.

Garadon picked up the freckled soldier's rifle. "He fired, that's good. Should be two more shells in this, I think." Now he had a rifle in each hand, ready to fire.

Time knelt, then stood, sweeping his arm and shouting, "Follow me!" He charged ahead just as the Union troops turned and fled toward the river. Time's first step was onto the lifeless arm of Rolen, with Stone beside him facing the sky with glassy sightless eyes. Time inhaled in shock, but kept moving.

The Rebels cheered lustily, believing they had routed the Union forces. Time told his boys to hold fire, acknowledging that only he and Garadon, and four boys, the youngest boys, were still alive from his platoon. And Knox would not leave his side. Even though the sister unit to his right was fairly intact, it was losing a soldier for every step just before a Union artillery barrage tore through every Rebel unit in sight. The smoke prevented a clear view but could not mask the imagined wreckage.

The carnage was massive. Time instinctively and immediately told his men to drop even when he knew the correct execution would be to keep moving forward.

He saw that going ahead would be useless; even though the Union soldiers had retreated, and that one deadly volley had decimated his platoon, other blue coats were peppering the field with effective rifle fire.

The crash and thunder of the Union artillery was having a ruinous effect on the Rebel charge. What moments before were the hollers of enthusiasm and victory were now the screams and lamentations of the dying. The ground trembled. Some of the fire was simple cannonball, but most were buckshot canister or fuse devices, deadly instruments no matter where they landed.

To get up and assault, especially at this pivot position, would be futile. To retreat directly was equally useless, too, as the concentration of artillery fire was too intense, and the smoke too thick, that fire from above or from friendly troops might kill them all.

Time saw in an instant that the only likely path to survival was onto the Yankee side, the west side, of the river. Time and Garadon both nodded to each other, and looked to the river on their left.

"Break to the river, boys, stay with me."

Time burst downhill toward the river bed, trying to judge a good spot near the ford that avoided where the Yankees were entrenched. As daylight was dying, a glimmer of broken rock and stone gave him what he wanted: a swift and shallow passage west across Stones River.

He hit the rocks at a sprint, resisting the impulse to turn and see who was behind him, knowing that if he stopped, they'd all stop, and he had to trust Garadon to do his job of picking up the rear.

Time hit the opposite shore, unchallenged, took ten long strides, stopped and looked back. Knox was right on his tail. "Keep moving, stay close to the river!"

Knox never broke stride, and bolted south using the sharp contour as cover. Time almost laughed aloud. Of course Knox can lead this, he knew; he's the company runner, doing what he does best.

Adam and Goff and Billy were next, following Knox at Time's urging. Garadon had a firm grip on the upper arm of a struggling Fish, who was uninjured but hopelessly winded. Time took the trail position, and Fish shook off Garadon only to be replaced by Time. The boy ambled forward in shame and resignation. Garadon noted that other Rebels were fleeing in the same general direction, both to his left and right.

Knox knew where he was going, and used the sharp decline toward the river to his advantage. He could not sprint, at the risk of losing his followers, but knew instinctively that cover and concealment was often as good, if not better, than speed.

He was wrong, today. Time could hear rifle fire directed at him, dirt flying and tree bark and branches snapping. He didn't think it came from the river, but from his direct rear.

"Faster, boys, faster, we're bein' pursued!"

"No crap, sergeant!" Garadon fairly laughed out loud, lifted Fish by his collar, and hurtled him forward so that the boy's foot struck the ground only every other step. Time grabbed the second rifle from Garadon's hand, stopped, turned, and fired two rounds and then one misfire at shoulder level in the direction of his pursuers. A scream. A shout of hot anger. Time dropped the spent weapon and raised his own, an Enfield with several rounds still loaded. He paused, and then emptied it in rapid succession when he heard the movement continue. Another scream, and several other shouts and oaths of vengeance.

Must be a company size unit, Time thought. They'll move slower than us now!

Knox's pace was now fast and true, and Garadon had a better grip on Fish without holding the second rifle.

They moved amidst hollering and rifle fire at a reckless sprint for over a mile. Time kept them in sight, not thirty yards to his front. The group cut toward the river bed and stopped suddenly and crouched low.

Time knew they had not stopped to rest, and saw the boys huddled around Knox behind a large protruding boulder.

"What's wrong?"

Knox was blinking sweat away rapidly. "We should cross here, but it's too deep in parts, and some of our boys have already tried it and been shot at by...them."

Knox pointed across the river, as attacking Union troops were pushing Breckinridge's entire command back to the assembly point of just an hour before. The whole attack had been a disastrous waste. All of it.

The Union forces in pursuit were now within fifty yards. There were a dozen Rebel soldiers just below them, closer to the water, trying to decide whether to chance the deep part of the river. They look as bad as we do, thought Garadon.

A crash through the brush to Time's immediate left, and three Union soldiers, teeth bared, eyes bright with the hunt, were upon them.

The first, a burly Yankee, brandished two pistols, pointing them directly at Garadon, who had no time to shoulder his rifle. The Yankee fired, both rounds missed, and at the same instant Adam Moas thrust his bayonetted rifle into the soldier's abdomen. The burly Yankee's face made a perfect oval, and he tried to back away, dropping his guns. Adam stood, leaned forward, and twisted his rifle a quarter turn as blood and grease flowed forward down the rifle barrel. The big man's size worked against him, and his momentum and weight pushed the blade in beyond the hilt. In a panic, Adam fired once, unnecessarily. The Yankee hit his knees, and

Adam pitched forward as he was dragged down by the dead soldier.

The second Yankee came in right behind the first, but struggled to keep his bearing as he was wrestling with a large campaign flag, a Confederate one. Time tackled the soldier, who reeked of whiskey, and the drunk Yankee fell to his knees clutching the flag. Time was too close to fire his weapon, but turned his empty rifle in a tight brutal arc and thrust the butt of it up perfectly into the jaw of the fallen Yank, whose head snapped back awkwardly and with finality. He was dead before he fell backward, still clutching the souvenir flag.

The third Yankee soldier was more assured, stepping into the circle of Rebels, and placed his bayonetted rifle point at Garadon's throat.

"Don't move, Johnny Reb." His face had tears of blood and sweat and his eyes appeared unfocused, as if running through the dense winter brush had ripped his face or scratched an eye, or both. He breathed heavily and was getting his bearings, looking back and forth between his two fallen comrades before him, one prone with a boy struggling beneath him, one facing the sky whose jaw and neck were bent absurdly. He stared back to the point of his bayonet and Garadon's face, seeing a larger Rebel, too late, start to bring his rifle butt down to his chest.

The Yankee knew he was a dead man, having walked into his own ball of Rebel snakes. He stepped forward once quickly to recoil his arms and thrust the bayonet into the half sitting half kneeling Garadon's neck, when a large knife whisked by Time's head, suddenly protruding from the open eye of the Yankee just before he could make a death stroke. He dropped his weapon, Garadon grabbing the barrel. Time froze, in awe of the large knife embedded firmly in the Yankee's eye socket.

The last Yankee moved his head left, then right, and faced the gray sky through the winter trees, as if hearing something of interest or amusement and did not know from where it came. He exhaled, loudly and slowly, his knees buckled, and he fell hard, dead.

Knox jumped on the fallen Yankee, turned the knife as if cleaning it on a rock, and pulled it with ungraceful force from the dead man's head. "I've been practicing."

Crashes and shouting around them, the Rebel group in Time's command frozen in wonder.

Fish sobbed, "What flag is that?"

Garadon blinked, shook his head, and said, "Tennessee, not sure which."

"Leave it," said Time, looking back into the woods for more Union troops. He could hear them but not see them. Other Confederates had engaged the company chasing them. Time guessed they had enough time to cross the river, right now. "Nice work, Knox."

"Not supposed to throw your knife," piped Goff, with forced laughter, "Eh, Corporal Garadon?"

"There's always exceptions, son. Sergeant?"

"C'mon. We're not gonna live forever, and we can't stay here! On me! We cross!" Time raged with a booming yell, and darted for the river. His cry spurred all the Rebels, and his boys and all Confederate soldiers within earshot crashed into the first part of the water.

@@@

It was a rout.

The freezing stream swelled in spots, and Time knew that the shallow sections ran quick and choppy, slippery rocks hidden from view, dangerous and hazardous on the run. The still, smooth water should be avoided. He continued shouting, the quick-seasoned soldiers running pell-mell, the youngest ones orbiting him. Time realized that when he stopped to shout at the remains of the company, the orphans, too, stopped running. It would be fatal for all of them to stop again at the stream culvert, so he plunged into it at a sprint, shouting, "*RUN!*"

Goff and a weaponless Adam raced each other ahead of Time, guessing where they could go, assuming correctly that the larger trees would provide adequate cover before they could reach fortified positions. Billy followed closely behind Time, as Fish sought the smooth part of the stream. He ran to the deepest part, a dark pool that invited him as all the others were splashing and running over rocks and fast water.

In two steps Fish was gone, under the surface.

Adam saw it happen, and assumed that Fish was swimming his way through the pool.

Garadon saw it out of the corner of his eye, and started to jump into the still smooth water, when two rifle rounds peppered the knee high water around him. He froze, waiting for the kill shot, and then in two exaggerated strides leapt feet first near where Fish went down. He disappeared.

In the next instant the water churned with a fury known only in a man's nightmares. Garadon's head broke the surface, and he struggled to stay afloat, both his arms working and his rifle now gone. He turned on his back and side-stroked his way to where he had started his jump, and his feet found purchase and he stood, shaking, and turned to the Union advance in a rage, shouting profanities and a vow to kill them all. Two, three rounds peppered the stream around him. He never wavered, shaking his fists in frustration and anger and grief. Garadon turned and started running bow-legged to the opposite bank, weaponless. Fish was gone.

The platoon kept running, every man for himself, and now all had broken through and started up the embankment, to the previous night's fighting positions. Time was not confident the holes would hold, assuming an artillery barrage would finish them if the infantry decided not to cross the ford. He silently prayed the makeshift breastworks would give way just enough if they found the right seams to cut through on the run.

A corporal from another unit of the 6th, a man of few words, was losing ground running up the hill, and even though the snap of bullets hitting trees and the zip of them passing became more urgent, he sat at the base of a large pine and stuck his feet in the air. The cold water ran out of his boots in a *whoosh*, and just as quick he was up and running, now with renewed spirit and much greater speed.

Time saw this, and started to imitate the motions at the same tree, when a rapid succession of *whiz-snap*, four or five times around him, had him scrambling back up and running. As he looked back he saw Garadon now on his own back letting the water pour out of his boots. They nodded to each other, Time's eyes pleading with his friend to hurry.

An anguished cry, from a child far from a man, stopped Time before he could make it to safety through a cut in the breastworks. He turned back again to face the river. Billy lay prone, struggling with his arms, the back of his left leg a mass of blood, bone, and shredded skin and uniform. He fidgeted mightily to grasp his utensils, to undo the pocket that held them.

Time moved to Billy, the sound of bullets whirring slowing down, the anger and pain and fright of the boy now a high pitch of dread that cut through the smoke and pierced straight through Time's senses. Billy was trying to examine and count the utensils, fingers moving slower by the second, and he met Time's gaze as the sergeant fell next to him.

"Don't move, son. Stop fussing."

"Sergeant Time!" Billy coughed, screamed, and tears flowed. "Take, take these." He thrust the pocket of cutlery at Time's face, then dropped his head and arm, exhaling quickly, softly, finally.

Another *whiz* and *snap*. Several more, one striking the expired boy. Time grabbed the cutlery and darted up the hill, seeing Goff and Adam beckoning to him from an angle in the breastworks, a perfect position to breach and continue running. He moved to them woodenly just as Garadon was at his elbow, gripping his upper arm in a vice. The whine of artillery can be heard in the last few seconds before impact and Time took one step before Garadon pushed him face first into the soft earth. The first rounds hit the streambed, stopping the Union advance, and for one brief second Time thought they might just make it, as the stupid Union bastards dropped hell on their own men.

Time looked up, smiled and winked at the eager faces of Adam and Goff, both wide-eyed with terror and incredulity.

"Where's Fish?" yelled Adam.

Then two concussive flashes of white, sprayed dirt and wood and mist, then darkness.

Time was stunned, but his deep prone position, courtesy of Garadon's presence of mind, likely saved him from grave injury of concussion or shrapnel. He shook dirt from his head, spat moss from his mouth and wiped his eyes with his coat sleeve. Ears ringing, he knelt, shaking his head and shoulders, and as he rose he saw the inert form of Garadon beside him. The sight did not register in his head yet. He looked up the hill to where the breastworks were, an oasis of safety as he remembered, but the trees, the breastworks, and the boys, Adam and Goff, were gone.

The artillery barrage was brief and horrific, no longer than a flash rainstorm, less than a minute. Time could not discern the direction it came from. He recalled Adam and Goff calling out, reaching for him, yelling, asking... something.

Time shook his head again. The ringing would not subside, but the sense of safety, the thing being ended, was profound. He stood shakily, looked down toward the stream and saw many dead, both gray and blue. Mostly blue, and many older soldiers, real soldiers. A few gray coated boys.

He looked up the hill again, vaguely aware that Garadon was stirring at his feet. The breastworks were gone. The ringing in his ears gave way to moans and cries of pain. Time turned again to go downhill, and stepped on a hand, on the outstretched arm of Billy, who was stone-still in death.

He remembered Adam's cry, "Where's Fish?" and started to go downhill to look for him, knowing that Fish never made it this far. Time squinted, seeing the stream now cratered unnaturally, its course changed forever. He thought he saw the boy, Fish, a form too small face-down in the middle of where the stream should have been. He looked at his own hands: his left clutched the satchel of utensils, his right bloody from trying to stanch the flow from Billy's leg wound.

Time's anger welled slowly, and he strode up the hill, stepping over what minutes ago had been a formidable breastworks, not perfect, but one that would have afforded cover and a punishing downhill field of fire. The painful ring in his ears was waning in pitch by the second.

It was now just sticks and mud. He didn't need to guess where the cut was before, or where the Moas brothers and several other frightened orphan soldiers had hid behind what was believed a safe haven from the threat of Union gunfire.

Two, perhaps three, direct artillery hits within a thirty foot area had decimated at least a dozen soldiers, now shattered and scattered remains. No movement. No sounds. Time heard a metallic click, again and again as his hearing improved, and whirled around twice, whipping his head back and forth before he realized he was gripping, grinding and mashing the utensils roughly in his hand. No other sounds. Even the moaning stopped.

Garadon stood, then bent and picked up Billy's rifle, checking its action and ensuring a round was chambered. It had not been fired.

Sporadic gunfire in the distance, which could mean two things, even this late in the day. Either a cessation of attacks for the day, or, much worse, a regroup of forces with one more assault in their hearts, the calm before another storm of waste.

Time closed his eyes and breathed deeply, inhaling the smoke of timber and powder, feeling the moisture from his cold sweat and the mist of blood in the air. He felt his wet freezing feet.

From his observations over the last few days he guessed the Union was reinforcing its gains, and that the combination of effective artillery and skilled maneuver over terrain had caused the rout. He still did not understand why the Rebel army did not stay in fortified positions, why it had taken an initiative to attack when they had a distinct advantage after the first day, why it put the railhead at risk, unnecessarily.

"It was all too easy for them. To hit here," Garadon said aloud, to himself, but it mirrored what Time was thinking. He wondered silently how the Union had known the precise position that provided escape for the Rebels, and where the breastworks, the last effective defensible position for the Confederates, was arranged.

Garadon thought of luck, stupid luck, but didn't believe in it. "More than luck," he said to the sky.

"I am glad you're okay, corporal."

"That was hellish, Jim. I thought I could help that boy, Fish. I..." He sighed heavily and shook his head in resignation.

The loud neighing of a huge steed, commanding in and of itself, at the point just where the breastworks had been. Breckinridge sat high, shoulders back, but his normally regal bearing was unravelling as he looked into the pit where the boys had been.

"My orphans! My poor orphans!" His anger mixed absurdly with tears and a coughing fit, giving the impression of a weeping, bereft man, a commander too emotional to grip the situation. Two timid captains rode behind the general, and Time recognized Dayton, the adjutant. They shook their heads, and clucked to each other in whispers.

General Breckinridge turned his horse quickly and expertly, and spat at them in disgust, his rage building, his eyes red and rimmed with tears of frustration.

"Fools! These were just boys! They should have been kept farther back! You, you idiots!" The captains actually cowered from the outburst.

Breckinridge pulled his horse away and cantered atop the tree line, surveying with mounting incredulity the devastation in the river bed. One of his officers called out, "General! Sniper fire!"

"Shut up! Oh my poor orphans! Oh, dear Lord, forgive me, forgive me! Just boys!" He hung his head in abject defeat, and his horse stopped.

Time strode with purpose to the general.

"By your leave, sir. Allow me to walk you through to inspect."

Breckinridge looked at Time, snorting with ire and astonishment, recognized him and nodded his assent. Time looked at the shocked captains, who had separated, and then looked to Garadon. The corporal nodded and made a line for the mounted officers, knowing he would have to get help from them to account for the dead and attend any wounded. Time turned the general toward the southeast, away from the carnage.

"Sergeant Time."

"Yes, general."

"We did our best, yes?"

"Yes, sir."

"But it wasn't good enough. We throw our children at hardened U.S. soldiers and expect... what?"

Time had no answer, and coughed in reply, dirt spewing from his nostrils.

The general's anger had not subsided, and he threw his head back and raged once more.

"*My orphans!*"

@@@

7
After the Fight

The sweep of the injured and the dead continued into the darkness, and the word came quickly that as soon as all soldiers were accounted for the company would move south and east and stay far away from the Union's now entrenched position around Stones River.

Time had only two men left, of his initial twenty five: Corporal Garadon, and the half-Indian Knox, who had fallen in a ditch and was still, hours later, covered completely in mud. Both were seasoned veterans and knew Time's silence was less remorse and reflection, and more trying to piece together the next move, the right thing to do now, in the face of orders, but mostly to be effective in the absence of them.

The shadow of twilight had died long before to complete blackness, and the glow of random fires crept to the tree line where the three men sat. They viewed the rings of hasty, smoky fires, as cold soldiers tried to stay warm in their wet uniforms. Many soldiers will stay cold and wet unless forced to strip and get dry.

Garadon and Knox had collected enough aged wood to take care of the three of them, but knew instinctively not to light it, not just yet. Knox had already stripped off his trousers, coat, boots and socks, and left Time's presence to get warm at an adjacent fire. Time breathed through his nose, the blue white plumes forced out as if the last part of daylight.

That's when Time saw him. There was a flicker in the near distance, along the tree line. The wind shifted slightly, into Time's face, and he thought he saw a rock move, then realized it was a squatting man who had moved to avoid fire smoke which had drifted oddly and stayed close to the ground. As the figure moved, the fire had brightened, and the clear face of the shaved trader glowed for an instant.

He was writing, furiously, on a small plank not forty yards away. He might be doing something else, Time mused, but it was an odd practice for someone who bragged that he could not read or write. Mother Corn was writing something with speed and confidence, glancing left and right as he scratched his pencil on the plank, which fluttered with paper.

He looked up from the wood plank and paper, and with an unusual sense, looked right at Time and Garadon, and visibly shuddered.

Garadon saw it, too, and was on his feet at a sprint in a second, covering the 40 yards to Mother Corn in less than it took for Time to take five strides, or for the trader to protest. Garadon wrenched the writing board from the man's grasp.

Time was there, now. "A map," said Garadon, handing it to Time.

Mother Corn hissed, "It's just a drawing."

"With words and contours and units and casualty numbers. You'll burn in hell for this."

Garadon quickly stuffed his favorite handkerchief into Mother Corn's mouth, preventing an outburst from the spy.

"Jim, this is what he's been doing. Marking our position and telling the enemy. A filthy spy. This turd is a filthy spy and he killed all our boys."

Time grabbed the back of the trader's neck, pushing him roughly to the ground. He looked over the terrain, away from the thick woods. It appeared that no one saw them. Garadon stamped on the small fire, and tossed in a couple hands-full of dirt for good measure. Too much moonlight and stars in a partial sky, so the darkness of the woods beckoned. Garadon picked up the writing board and paper.

"We'll need this as evidence, so he can be properly tried."

Time was in a foul humor and saw nothing to discuss. With his grip firmly on Mother Corn's neck, he thrust the spy into the tree line, taunting, "Be quiet, now."

Garadon looked out and saw no response to the small crash in the brush, and when he turned back both Time and the trader were gone in the darkness. He listened, and followed the thrashing steps.

Mother Corn's wagon was right there, a dozen yards into the tree line, well concealed in the decaying brush. Time reached into it, felt for a few moments, and found what he needed. With a furious grip still on the neck of the bent over spy, Time pushed and dragged him farther into the dense wood, trees shorn of leaves, though the icy tendrils of the cowed branches reflected some ambient light. Garadon followed wordlessly, glancing left and right repeatedly, and once or twice behind him.

Mother Corn started to moan into the gag, and wretched into it in a spasm. Time stopped and pulled the gag out. The trader started to protest, but Time would have none of it.

"One sound, just one, and you hang. Here. Slowly. I have some questions for you."

Garadon suspected there would be few questions.

Time pushed Mother Corn face-first to the ground, glancing up and finding the tree he was looking for while jamming his foot in the small of the trader's back, pinning him to the ground. He looped a quick and efficient noose around the trader's neck, and with a snap pulled it tight enough to choke any loud sound but not cut off air supply.

Mother Corn wheezed.

Time looked up and tossed the rope expertly through a sturdy branch juncture of a healthy oak, the tail end of the rope keeping its coil as it nestled on the ground.

"This'll do the job. Corporal Garadon. Grab that end."

Garadon did not hesitate. He swung the excess rope behind him, cinching it to his waist. Time grabbed Mother Corn with both of his gnarled fists, shook the spy savagely and backed him to a large fallen tree.

"You told them where we were. The orphans." Time spat in Mother Corn's face. "They're *children*!"

Mother Corn's big and bloodshot eyes were wide with fear. "No, no, no, not here, never here."

"Liar," Garadon said with finality.

"You came back here, you scum. Most of 'em are dead. Why would you do that?" Time shook him with every word.

"They were gonna kill me!"

"Liar." Garadon had little sympathy.

"No, they wouldn't kill you. They'd pay you." Time forced his right hand into the coat pocket of the spy, and pulled out neatly folded paper. U.S. dollars, not the scrip of the confederacy.

"I, I, trade with everyone!" Mother Corn cried in fear.

Time yanked the spy to his full height, and lifted him to the fallen trunk's highest point, a yard off the ground. Mother Corn tried to stay crouched, knowing what his fate was to be.

Garadon leaned back, straightening the rope, making it taunt enough to stand the trader up to his toes.

"One last thing," whispered Time.

Garadon loosened the rope, and Mother Corn exhaled and stood firm on the fallen trunk, thinking he might still be reprieved or rescued by Time's reasonableness.

"Go to hell." Time pushed Mother Corn backwards, and Garadon yanked on his end and leaned back to the ground.

Mother Corn struggled for several long minutes, his windpipe crushed, the slipknot noose effective and tight, if not quite swift. The spy's eyes bulged and glazed a deep black. Time stared into the dead man's eyes whenever the slowly spinning and kicking body turned to face him. Garadon kept his vigil as anchor, but never looked up.

"What goes on here?" Knox had a blanket around his shoulders, but was otherwise still stripped.

Time continued looking at the hanged spy. "How long you been there?" Time sounded bored.

"What, what? Just now! Have you lost your senses, Time?"

Time spun on his heel and strode the few steps to the dry Knox, neck and hands still caked in dirt. Time went quickly up to his nose, and Knox nearly fell pulling away from him. Even in the dark Knox could see the menace in Time's soul.

"This garbage is a spy. Caught him drawing a map. He confessed. We hanged him," each word measured, even, final.

"You can't just hang him, Time."

"Sergeant Time to you, Knox."

"But, but, you'll both hang now!"

Garadon, fatigued, cold, and aching, said simply, "Shut up, Knox. He dead, sergeant?"

Time walked over to the now motionless cadaver. He took his hip knife out and drove it, hard, into

Mother Corn's leg, twisted it, and with a satisfied grunt pulled it out.

"Yeah, he's dead. Let it down."

"Dear God, what have you done?" Knox practically squeaked.

"Most of the company, and all of my platoon, except you," Time pointed his bloody knife at both men, "are dead. All boys. Children! This scum was a Union spy. We found him drawing a map. He confessed. We hanged him." He drew another breath, deeply, and exhaled in a wet white mist. "This was for all of them. This spy killed my orphans. For money. Killed our boys for profit."

Garadon stood, brushed his trousers off, sweating from exertion, and kept a casual expression on his face.

"He's in hell, Knox." To Time he said, "Now, I need a fire."

Knox ran out of the woods.

@@@

The next morning the camp routine revolved around ministering to the less than critical wounded and burying the dead, the surgeons working miles back from the battlefield unmolested by the Union forces. The Yankees did not pursue the defeated Rebels. Winter warfare had many disadvantages, and securing winter quarters and keeping soldiers from dying of sickness or deserting outright was more of an imperative than vanquishing the enemy.

Time and Garadon had left the carcass of Mother Corn right where he died, and then made their fire on the edge of the wood in plain sight of the rest of the encampment. They expected to be arrested that night, and wanted to be dry for it, stripping and warming their coats and trousers and socks and boots. The men remained silent, and their eyes met once and both soldiers chuckled at their nakedness in the cold. They used the trader's cart planks for their fire, a splendid roaring blaze that made quick work of the thawing job at hand.

The embers of the fire were still red-hot when Time and Garadon were awakened from a fitful sleep. Neither man had slept in the same tent at the same time for a week. Whispers, feminine and bird-like came from the wood line, away from any line of sight.

"Sergeant Time. Corporal Garadon."

Cloud walked to the rear of their pup tent, calling again. Time grunted, and said, "Yes."

Cloud beamed. "I cannot go further. I have food for you. Hot soup, with rabbit and squirrel and greens. Good greens, nice and thick, too."

Garadon burst from the tent clad only in undergarments, though his boots were on. The dawn air was cold, but the hot food was a blessing. After a quick hello to Cloud, he grabbed the pail. "Enough for us, Time. Enough for us."

Time emerged, alert and weary. Cloud's tentative cheerfulness told him all he needed to know.

Garadon sensed it, too. "Where's my Genevieve?"

"She's not your anything, corporal, and she's on the other side of the camp, with more soup, looking for her brothers."

Time had a blanket wrapped around his shoulders, and stared at Garadon wolfing down the hot food, allowing him his fill, first.

"Well. About that." Time could not meet her eye.

"Oh. Oh, no." Cloud sank to her knees. Time was too tired to help, and Garadon was too hungry to care.

"You have to get to Genny right away, Cloud."

"Where are their bodies?" She practically shrieked into her hands.

"Now, Cloud, they died quick. But terribly. There is not much remaining, except..."

She gripped her hair, sobbed, and remained still. Time could not look at her grief, and could not help it. He had spent all his grief in the woods not a hundred feet away hours before. He motioned for Garadon to give him the pail and spoon.

The corporal said, matter-of-factly, "It's good and hot, sergeant. Take it, take it. I got mine." As Time dug unto the stew, Garadon looked across the encampment, searching for Genevieve. He could tell her. He should tell her.

Time had a thought. "Cloud, I do have one set of table cutlery, you know, from Goff. He traded for them." The lie came easily, the image of Billy thrusting the small satchel at him vivid and fast.

He set the pail down, even though his stomach screamed for the nutrition. Time opened the pocket satchel, saw a cut in it, and counted three pieces. A teaspoon was missing. It must have slipped out, he thought, but where?

"Oh, damn."

Cloud stared at him, then the silver. "Oh, my. Oh. Miss Genny will need this, truly, Sergeant Time." She grasped the three pieces, knife, fork, and large spoon, into her folded hands.

"Thank you for saving these, sergeant. Thank you. God Bless you," she said to herself, remaining on her knees close to the tent's edge.

"I can't see her," said Garadon, to no one.

Time heard the steady footfall of several soldiers walking with purpose, crunching heedlessly through untrodden frozen grass and muck. He suspected this might be the arrest detail.

"Cloud, go, now. Walk, don't run. But go."

Breckinridge paced, alone, in a flat sparse area in the misty rain. He wore no hat, his shock of brown hair unkempt and his face unshaven. He was making the same circular movements in his solitary track, a personal parade deck that secured his private thoughts.

General Hanson had been killed in the assault the day before. It was a grave blow to Breckinridge's Brigade and the depth of leadership in Bragg's command. Hanson led from the front, and paid for it. Breckinridge could not help but speculate that if Hanson had not been struck down, the tide of battle may have favored the south.

Nonsense, Breckinridge mused. Hanson was right in the first place. The whole assault was a fool's errand. A complete waste.

The situation with the alleged spy was a nuisance. The evidence brought to him was damning to Mother Corn, and an embarrassment to all the officers, including himself, who accepted the merchant's presence as benign. But the breach of protocol after the battle had cooled by Sergeant James Time was inexcusable. The accomplice, a corporal, was no better, but every indication was that Time ordered Garadon to hold the rope.

I would have held it, too, thought the general. I would hold it right now if given the opportunity.

Damn that spy. And damn this war.

"Excuse me, sir." Captain Dayton interrupted tactfully.

"Yes, captain."

"Sir, one of General Bragg's staff has questioned both Time and Garadon. I suspect he will recommend courts martial for both."

"And?" This was not a surprise to Breckinridge. Bragg's heavy handedness with his own was well established, and a subordinate would acquiesce to whatever Bragg was inclined to want. Stupid, and borderline cowardly, though likely prudent to the ambitious and career minded.

"My opinion only, sir. General Bragg will execute them, definitely Sergeant Time, who insists it was all his doing."

"I think you're right." Breckinridge started pacing again, running through his mind how to approach Bragg, and how to appeal to him to spare these soldiers. Survivors are heroes, he could say, they fought to live, and will fight again for the Confederate States. Yes, he thought. Survivors are heroes.

@@@

"I have to make a run for it, Garadon. I won't hang for killing that scum."

Garadon was aloof. "They'll probably just shoot you."

Time snorted. "Me? What about you?"

"I was following orders, sergeant." They both laughed quietly.

Each man was chained to a metal bar, separated from the southernmost tree line by a horse pen. Security for them was lax. No soldier had the spirit to abuse or hold high prison standards to Time, the platoon sergeant and the de facto commander of one of the fateful orphan platoons, nor the energy to take on Garadon, the quietly powerful and noted fierce fighter with crazy eyes and a ready smile. An ankle shackle only, one for each man, kept them from simply walking away. The command kept these two segregated from other petty prisoners, and they now had a full height tented roof over their heads. A side table was laden with normal soldier rations, but there was plenty of it, as fellow Rebels came by and left a portion of their personal allotment as an honorarium.

"Look at all this food."

Time laughed, "Yes, and even you can't eat it all."

The sergeant still carried his remorse, not for the murdered Mother Corn, but for the waste of the boy soldiers, his orphans, and even for the real agony he witnessed by his general, John Breckinridge. Time kept an eye out, through the horse pen, into the tree line. He expected to see Cloud and Genny before nightfall.

He was not disappointed. Time saw Genny, first, such a thin wan near-woman, face darkened in grief and anger. "There's our girl, Garadon, there's our girl."

Garadon rose and looked out of the tent opening with Time. He saw Genny and his heart jumped, and then he caught her eye. She tried to coax a smile from her mouth, but failed. Time held up both hands, mimicking and mouthing, "Wait, wait."

But Genevieve paid no heed, and walked deliberately around the makeshift horse kennel and directly to the slouching guard in front of the jailor's tent.

"I would like to bring food to your prisoners."

"No need, Missy, they have more than enough." He stood awkwardly and touched his cap. "The whole camp has been leavin' 'em food. I was gonna ask for some." He smiled crookedly, but stood taller remembering that he had the honor of being the jailor to the great Time and Garadon.

"Oh." Genny's courage was failing her in the face of this soldier's cheerfulness.

"Can you leave the basket here with me, Miss? I won't touch any food." He stood aside to let her pass into the tent.

Genny rushed to Garadon.

"I'm so glad," stifling a sob, "Oh, no." She collapsed. Her face looked old, stricken, her eyes red and rheumy from hours of grief, her nose raw.

Time was overwhelmed by her conflict of mourning and cheer. So these two do like each other, Time mused silently, but her sorrow over her lost brothers would be worn on her shoulders like a chained shawl, forever.

"I am so very sorry, Miss Genevieve. They," Time hesitated, knowing of her over-sensitivity, yet he plowed ahead, "they died most bravely, trying," he looked away, "to save young Billy."

Genny sat up abruptly hugging her knees, expression stern, the glare of her eyes piercing Time.

"I want them buried properly."

Garadon was compelled to speak up.

"Miss Genny, proper isn't really possible. We lost the fight, and the field, and lost badly. We'll all be leaving here soon."

"No, you won't." Her expression changed again, stone-like, and continued in a monotone. "Nor will we, Cloud and me. They're talking of building a monument, right away. The soldiers are piling rocks now, and headstones are being cut. I, I, I commissioned a carver to cut two stones for Adam and Goff."

"Where'd you get the money for that?" Asked Garadon, more incredulous than curious.

"I sold Cloud to that captain, General Breckinridge's adjutant or something. He guaranteed he'd see to it personally if she became his cook and groomer."

"What..." Garadon had little use or care for Cloud, but this was too much out of character for sweet Genevieve.

"And you have no intention of allowing that. You haven't thought this through, though, young lady." Time tried to suppress a smile of pride. He knew Genny would never part with Cloud, would rather die than sell her, but was determined to do right publicly by her brothers.

And Time knew their problem, his problem, was now all immediate, and would need to be acted upon within a day, perhaps just a few hours from now. He disliked the adjutant, on many levels. The orphan's blood was as much on his hands as Time's.

"Genny." Time knelt and held her hands in one of his, now eye to eye with both the girl and Garadon. "We need to leave."

"We?"

"I need to think about this, but we may need to depart tonight. Have the stones been commissioned already?"

"Yes, and in front of the general. He approved of it."

"Tonight it is." The fact that Breckinridge approved of the stones meant there would be no turning back, and the fact that the general also approved the sale of a slave under his nose was ignored. "This guard is on until almost ten this evening. The next guard will be tired from working all day. Can you and Cloud gather some provisions, and be at the north end of the corral, right," he pointed, "there, at midnight?"

"Yes, yes I think so."

"And blankets. We'll need four horses, too."

"No. Just three." Garadon said in a neutral tone.

Genny and Time stared at him. He held up a hand, and stood.

"I will stay here. They'll shoot you or hang you, Time, they will. Have to. You're a Yank, and nobody can go around hanging spies, especially without a hearing, or trial, or..."

"Inquiry."

Time began to see the reality.

"Yeah, that. I was following orders. Woulda done it anyway, but. Well, they won't hang me. And at dawn they'll need someone to say something, and I can stall 'em for quite a while. I'll talk it up with the guards. Give you a darn good head start." He paused and looked at Genny. "I've known some of these boys all my life, it seems. I can't desert 'em. And you wouldn't trust a man who did, Genevieve."

Time was touched, and impressed. He placed a paternal hand on Garadon's broad bony shoulders.

"You're a good soldier, Corporal Garadon."

"I'm a better soldier than you, Sergeant Time." He smiled. "I follow orders." They both snorted knowingly. "And I care for this girl more than you know. Please watch over her." Garadon could not bring himself to look at Genny, but just held her hand.

The solemnity of the moment amplified the external sounds of horses, soldiers fussing about, and the occasional barked command or curse. Scents were greater, too, as the softness of Genevieve and her natural beauty was overcome by the dank and acrid smells of men, horses and the constant cold and damp and periodic thaw.

"It'll be cold for many days and weeks, Genny. Gather only what we need to eat and sleep. Nothing else. If we have to throw away any material it'll leave a trail."

Garadon put his arm around Genny. "Where will you head to?"

"North, along the Appalachia."

@@@

The winter sky was thick at midnight, and starlight could not poke through. Cloud approached the soldiers, older men with injuries that prevented front-line work, who were watching the horses. The soldiers were cold, and rubbed at wounded limbs in pain and numbness both real and perceived.

"I want to exercise the horses. Captain Dayton will accompany me," she said, with authority.

The soldiers could not hide their derision.

"Of course, uh, what's your name?"

Everyone knew her name. The whole camp knew her as the pretty Genevieve's slave maid, now the property of the adjutant captain. The smaller minded assumed she was more than just a horse groomer. She was chattel, like the beasts in the corral.

"Cloud, young man," she said to the much older soldier, applying a new tack. "I'll probably be walking. He said to get three well-rested ones. There were many soldiers walking about at the house, they's yelling at each other, and the Cap'n told me to go fetch three." Cloud made her voice sing-song, almost coy. The mention of three also lent itself to their prurient imagination. She knew that with a little honey, she could get the best horses available. Cloud smiled.

The guards saw an opportunity for the second best thing, after hot food, in an armed camp awaiting movement.

Gossip.

"Well, Cloud, what're they jawin' about?"

Cloud launched into a discourse on everything from boots to balloons, and the soldiers were rapt with attention. She kept clutching her coat about her hips and throat, shaking her fist to the sky, and even feigned a "*whatwasthat*?" to an imaginary sound over her shoulder. In a minute the old salts were enthralled and captivated by the energy from this small woman.

"Well, now. Much obliged for the information. But, Cloud, what about..."

"What was that?" Cloud spun and looked due south, then straight up into the night sky.

"Nothin'. I didn't hear nothin'." From the sentry missing an ear.

The older soldier coughed. "Let's give her the horses, now. If they come lookin' for her, we'll have to stand all night. Miss Cloud?"

"Yessir?"

"Could you maybe bring the horses back yourself? We'd like to catch some sleep, one at a time, like."

"Oh, yes, I know. My bones are small and cold but you big men must be aching terrible so."

The soldiers fetched three fine rested horses, handing them over to the slave girl in silence.

Cloud walked the horses away, in a single file. She prayed that she and Genny would have as much easy fortune finding saddles.

Minutes earlier, Time crept from the tent as the single guard slept. The security of the separate jail had gotten more lax by the hour, as familiarity and respect from the prisoners was reaching mythic proportions in the camp. Both men had been unshackled before dark simply by asking.

With extra salt pork and some beef, hardtack, turnips and dried fruit stuffed in his pockets and carrying a sack and blankets, Time crouched and crawled to the closest tree line, advancing in bursts of several yards at a time, then listening, then advancing again when the trees did not protest. He watched as Cloud was talking to the corral guards, who looked like crippled men. Recognizing one, he suspected the guard would harass the black girl, as Time knew that the bitterness of the injured would be quickly displayed in a cruelty to one more cursed by fate than by injury.

Although Time couldn't hear Cloud, he observed her gesticulating with a fury and he was prepared to go on the offensive when he saw her posture change, as did the soldiers.

She was flirting. They were absorbed in her story telling.

Smart girl, thought Time. I wonder what fables she told.

He began moving closer as the soldiers secured three sinewy horses, healthy cavalry-types, and then helped her tie the bridles to each other. Time was less than forty feet away as Cloud started walking vaguely toward the command house, out of earshot of the sentries.

The lead horse snorted, and Time coughed with it. Three more snorts, and Time's coughs became more urgent, and then Cloud noticed, her relief obvious. They were now less than six strides apart, but they kept moving.

"Miss Genny is by the water pump. But we need saddles."

"Take the horses into the tree line until you can't see the camp. Stay with them. And take these." He handed her the blankets and the sack he was carrying.

Cloud did as she was told, praying silently. She stamped her feet absently, and looked inside the sack Time gave her. Vegetables. Salt beef and lots of pork. Dried fruit, and hardtack. Some of the best provisions in winter, usually reserved for officers. As the cold and damp leeched through her shoes she focused on the image of the dead trader as told to her, and what might have happened to the Moas brothers. They, too, were cold and dead and lonely somewhere in a mass grave. She and Genny would need this anxious sergeant to get to safety, away from her being owned outright, and the sergeant from a certain execution. An example is always made.

She heard footfalls, and the night snapped cold on the ragged earth as all sounds were amplified in the air near the horses. Then it deadened. Time and Genny came into view, the sergeant struggling with three saddles, a rifle, and a pistol.

"I'll get these on and we'll move out right away. Let me saddle the big chestnut, then you can secure the provisions as I move to the next," whispered Time.

"But, sergeant..."

"No talking, Missy. Just do."

@@@

"I have already heard, Captain Dayton. Bad news travels fast." Major General Breckinridge stood at noon the day after the escape, with his uniform tunic collar open, outside his temporary command tent. He looked haggard. The open collar was not in character with his normally proud bearing in public.

"General, that Garadon character, Corporal Garadon, had been beaten and nearly smothered by his own account." Dayton paused, and had difficulty meeting Breckinridge's stony glare. Both men knew that Garadon was fiercely loyal to Time. Garadon's tall tale made little sense, and the command assumed that the sentries at the corral, the prison tent, and the saddlery tent had cooperated through negligence or outright collusion. All pled ignorance, and threats of incarceration or worse were met with hollow icy stares.

"And?" Breckinridge looked up into the cold gray sky.

"And I don't know, sir. I just don't. I have ordered a three man party to hunt down Sergeant Time and the three horses. And those two women." Dayton seethed with the indignation of the righteous victim.

"No, captain. No. We will not waste resources chasing them actively. Forget the women, too."

"But, sir! I've already paid the stone carver! It's public knowledge!"

"Easy, captain. Your money is forfeit. Your reputation and honor are much more important. Your ego will recover." Breckinridge placed a paternal hand on Dayton's shoulder. "And after the corporal recovers from his, uh, injuries, please find him a suitable assignment, out of what's left of my division. His popularity is too much of a distraction. If one more officer comes to me vouching for those two men..." Breckinridge shook his head slowly back and forth. "The First Brigade took over fifty percent casualties two days ago. The survivors are too hardened to care about legalities. I want the entire sordid mess behind us."

Dayton slumped. "No charges, sir?"

"No charges. I'll deal with General Bragg."

@@@

Part Three

Exodus

...There shall be no harm or ruin on all my holy mountain...

Isaiah 11:9

8
A Savior

After a night and a day the three had barely spoken, acutely aware of the enormity of the weight of their respective fate and role in the world. A deserter, a fugitive slave, and a pregnant thief, all of who had lost dear brothers.

Moving north-northeast, Time estimated that they had made a respectable distance of thirty miles. Feeding and watering the horses was crucial to their run north, and every opportunity to do both needed to be taken with a minimum of risk. After eighteen hours of riding, with no sleep beforehand, they were all exhausted, man and beast. Time made a fire, while Genny covered herself in blankets under the pines. Cloud stood with Time, too tired to do anything but rub emerging sores. Time was morose.

"You did everything you could, Sergeant Time. You didn't kill them. Every minute they had that day was because of you."

"I don't know about that, Miss Cloud. I will mourn them all the days of my life."

"You're a changed man, I think."

Time eyed her, aware that her perceptiveness and sensitivity to his condition were not traits he was accustomed to seeing in anyone since he was a boy.

"Cloud, when a soldier dies, we mourn two lives. We mourn the life he had before, and the life he will never live. Been that way forever, I suspect." He paused, swallowed, and pushed on. "When an orphan dies, we mourn the life he wishes he could have led, of the comfort of knowing he is loved mightily, and always has a place to call home."

Cloud's head drooped, and snapped back upright. "Dear me, sergeant. I must rest now."

"Good night, young lady."

Cloud smiled. "And good night to you, kind sir."

@@@

After another day of riding north, and another fire, they set up a proper camp with blankets as tenting. Genny as yet had not spoken more than a yes or no. Time asked questions to draw the girl out, but was met with silence or tears. He looked to Cloud to assist, but when he questioned her, she was just as recalcitrant. Grief, he thought. We each come to our own peace, if ever.

The next night, after a rough ride with cold and murky weather amidst threatening skies, they made camp and managed cooking a meal and drinking coffee. Their travel elevation was improving, and even without a map it was evident their exodus was not going to put them in contact with organized units of soldiers. Marauders would be their downfall.

Cloud and Time stared into the dying embers of the fire. Genny had retired.

"You have asked about me about my family. I barely remember them. Can you tell me about yours?"

"Not much to tell, Cloud."

"Honestly." Not a question, though Cloud raised one eye disapprovingly. "Not taken from your family as a baby, hmmm?"

"Too much to remember," he sighed.

Cloud stayed silent, but kept her eyes on Time's bent head, which changed shapes and colors and contours, as he added kindling and poked the fire. The flames snapped at a hardened nut, the red glow seeking fuel to stay alive. An orange thread melted below the surface of ash beginning to cool as the coals touched the night air.

Time breathed smoke in, held it, and exhaled in a large cough.

"I think of a girl constantly."

Cloud was startled by the admission, inhaled sharply, but made no sound.

"She was delightful. Her smile carried sunlight. Her eyes blinked and winked and opened just for me."

"Oh dear! Is she gone?"

Time laughed lightly and smiled. "Oh, no, I think not. She's my brother's wife."

"Oh. Oh, dear."

His smile was wistful and he met her open-mouthed stare. Time coughed a terse laugh.

"Not what you think, Cloud Parker. We were children, then, not yet 14 years old, as young as the boys." It pained him, thinking of Adam and Goff. "I was starting to get into more trouble than I should have. Jon is less than a year younger than me, but more intelligent, more serious, more committed. He's quiet, he's thoughtful. Then and now, more mature."

"More quiet than you?" Cloud couldn't suppress her incredulity.

"He, well, kept to himself, a man of few words. Jon is ambitious, well-read like you, but keeps his opinions to himself. Above all he was most obedient to our father, while I was, well, difficult." Time poked the embers again with a stick he held, then snapped it in two and tossed the pieces on the cooling ash, much of it blacker than the night. A few sparks rose in protest.

"Jon went to West Point, did I tell you that?" Time saw Cloud shake her head no. "He's an army officer, a colonel now. He's regular army. I've heard this... well, I haven't seen him since many years before the war started."

The night was suddenly brighter as a cloud moved away from the partial moon, which now shined like a beacon over the trees, bathing them in a soft light. They both looked up. Time smiled.

"I think I'll find him now. First, we'll get to Pennsylvania, at least, and get you and Genny settled. Then I'll enlist and ask for his unit."

"Will you be arrested?"

"I think not. I have skills, and you don't arrest volunteers. Jon's respected, a professional. Many of his peers know me. It's where I should have been from the start, and now I mean to make it right, as much as I hate it all."

Cloud saw several dry sticks nearby in the new light of the moon. She moved quickly to grab them, stripped the dry leaves with a practiced hand, and stuck them into the center of the coals. A snap, the smell of wet burn, and a modest flare licked hungrily up to consume the tinder.

"Why do you think of the girl?" Cloud's feminine curiosity would not be distracted, and she enjoyed listening to this complicated man.

"Jon's wife, now. Everyone loved her. She had only eyes for him, though, and he was smart enough to return her favor, and protect it from mischief. I left home at seventeen rather than follow in my father's ambition for me, to go to the Point. Been rough-necking and living hand to mouth for over twenty years. Lived the lives of a dozen different men. I wouldn't trade it for anything, except, maybe..."

"Except her?"

"She was the last person I spoke to before I left. I told her I loved her. She said she loved me back."

The fire snapped in rapid succession. Time inhaled sharply, turning away from Cloud and grasping at imaginary kindling. He turned back to the fire with loose brush and grass in his hands, and threw it on the softening coal. It smoked, burning in a wet sizzle.

"But not that way," she said, with little sympathy.

"Aye. Not that way."

@@@

By the fifth night their routine was the same. Genny sought dry wood and managed the limited food supply, Time made camp, and Cloud tended to the horses' feeding and grooming. Once the fire was started, they were able to rest, physically, if not mentally. Time provided the entertainment, usually conversation about himself, which tended to take the girls away from their own crippling grief. Their fire tonight was high and bright, and their circle was tighter.

I will not look away from him, thought Cloud. He won't meet my eye, but if he does, I will not look away. Time kicked at an imaginary object.

"I was a grave disappointment. Drank much. As I bounced around first New Jersey, then New York City, my brother Jon began to emerge into the man everyone wanted him to be, wanted me to be. Jon went to West Point and excelled. I crashed stupidly into petty crime and sloth. 'Oh, but for the Grace of God,' I'm alive now."

"But you have many talents, sergeant. You have mastered soldier skills. You have led many in battle, and they looked up to you, officers and men alike. You speak well, so you must remember much of your education. None of these traits are accidental."

Time looked up, and Cloud held her stare, a challenge to him.

"No. Not accidental. Acquired by training and a nurturing family. And squandered. Wasted. I have spent most of the past two decades avoiding what caring people tried to cultivate."

"But they must know…"

"They're all gone, except Jon, and his bride and brood. Wonderful people, all, from what I have managed to learn."

Time smiled, and Cloud returned it in the darkness. The horses neighed.

"My people were Catholic. You?"

Cloud brightened. "No, we have our Savior, thank you."

"No offense meant, Cloud, just asking, not prying."

"You do not worry me anymore, sir. I can tell a man of faith…"

"Pshaw." Time cringed, but amused.

"And you are one. You have kept the good of your people, I think, even after so many years.

"Good. And thank you."

"Do you know God has a plan for you?"

Time pretended to ignore the usually silent girl.

Genny pressed on. "I do not know mine, sergeant, but I can see yours. Maybe it's just to be here, right now, to help me and Cloud."

"It can't be to kill boys or watch them be killed. I won't do it anymore."

"But you'll protect us, now?

"Of course, Miss Genny, of course."

Genevieve stepped up to Time, and clasped his hands, coaxing him easily to rise. She placed his hands on his chest, her tiny fingers barely covering them, and pressed firmly.

"Hear you heart, Sergeant Time. You can't help but to do the right thing." Her eyes smiled, her face serene and confident. Time's shoulders sagged.

"They were my soldiers, my orphans. I failed."

Genny gripped his hands with vigor. "They were my orphans, too. I will always look after them now, in my dreams."

"Who will look after you?"

"The Lord watches me."

@@@

Genny was becoming bolder talking to this soldier, a man who deserted to protect her and who knew the risks of transporting a girl who would become heavy with child, who was trying with futility to rescue a friend from a life of slavery, and who challenged the winter.

"You are complicated, Sergeant Time." Genevieve tried to sound casual.

Time adjusted the horse blanket on the light brown mare, ignoring the girl.

"You are different when not around your kind, around soldiers. You are different around women."

"No, I am not." Time's exasperation was evident. "I just have seen too much death." He rested the crown of his head on the horse's back, suddenly fatigued.

Genny whispered, "Are you ready to die?"

"No," he groaned, immobile.

"You have to be ready, Sergeant Time. Once you die, you either live forever or you don't."

Time lifted his head and fixed her stare.

"I know that ruse, Miss Genny. Dead is dead. You can't live forever, which has kept me alive this long, knowing that."

"If you embrace the Savior, you'll live forever, through Him!"

Time could not help but to smirk guiltily at Genny, this sad girl who lost both parents, her only brothers, and was with child and with no husband, yet still possessed the fervor of her faith, a faith that should have weakened long before. But, he thought, her belief is unshakeable. She is convinced, as his own mother was long, long before.

"Well, I hope they have girls in heaven." Time said, flatly. Genny smiled back at him.

"It's not like that, sergeant, and I know you know it. Remember breakfast today? Like that."

Time's amusement was now more pleasurable. Breakfast had included marmalade.

"Miss Genny, your joy of life, the sheer bounty of small things, just collides with the decay of it all, and the decay of our spirit that surrounds us in our desperation."

Her smile vanished.

"No, James Time. Decay is dust. It is not life eternal." She started to walk away, but instead turned and faced Time fully over the horse's back. Genny would not look away from the man, and after staring at Genny's forehead for a long minute, Time pressed out the blanket, nodded, and turned, ensured the beast was hobbled, and walked away without a good night.

@@@

9
Rock Chapel

The trio had been moving steadily northward for over two weeks, and their supplies were dwindling.

Genevieve, Cloud, and Time trudged up the narrow path, Time in front giving his own horse its lead. The beasts were sure-footed, Genny's mount strong, with Cloud's sometimes trying to pass the work horse. The slope was moist, and the dawn departure from camp was a matter of Time's fear and deep intuition. The more distance from the base of the ridgeline, from Tennessee and the valleys of Virginia, the less likely they would be caught.

And Time would avoid the noose, both as an accused murderer and now as a deserter.

The going was slow, and the cross-cut path was easy on the horses' legs but made the trip longer. The ridgeline became steeper, and hours later the sun bore down without heat and the path cut back down the hill, then forked.

"It's up or down," said Time, looking at the sky.

"I don't feel well." Genny's head hung.

"We can rest, Gen." Cloud affirmed.

The women dismounted, and obligingly stretched. There was ample grass at this point of the foothills of

Appalachia, and the horses fed, having drank their fill not an hour before.

Time was weary but restless. "The wider path is downhill. Maybe a town or small settlement camp. They can't be trusted, at least not yet. We go up."

Genny was too tired to look up the slope. The path was narrower, dense with overgrowth, and appeared not to have been used in months.

Cloud sensed Genny's agitation and fatigue. "There may be a reason for the disuse, sergeant. Perhaps there's a hermit up there, a recluse."

"Perhaps. But he's getting company tonight."

"Is it all right to eat something?" Genny whined.

"Of course, Genny, but just a little."

Time looked at Cloud with disapproval.

"I think wherever we stay tonight, we'll not be there for long." He paused and pointed at Cloud, and then up at the sky. "Now's a good time to pray, Cloud Parker."

@@@

The January cold tingled the hair on their covered heads. A grayness linked the now near barren trees, trees that looked like shredded earth hanging as drapes to the ground. The trunks appeared brittle, and seemed to move in the bitter cold. The path was for one at a time, and they continued silently in a single file, the only sound the snort from the horses' snouts as they exhaled in fierce translucent plumes. The slope was angled and unforgiving, the foot purchase only made secure by the will of the horses as they leaned their heads upward and forward.

They continued to rise, gradually and imperceptibly, the sun hidden behind the gray winter sky, as it had been for many days. The forest thinned and began to show the light of a modest summit.

"Look," from Genevieve, who had been silent all day.

Time abruptly stopped. "Where? What?" The urgency of confrontation in his thin voice.

"Down there," as she pointed. Cloud dismounted and stared.

"That's a house."

If not for the reflection of a stray tin cup, the shack would have remained unseen. One door, one grimy window, but even at fifty yards and surrounded by evergreens the gun slats in the structure were unmistakable.

"No fire. Looks abandoned. Stay here." Time dismounted, rifle at the ready, and walked down the slope toward the shack.

"Be careful," blurted Genny. Cloud looked at her, then at Time. She suppressed a laugh as Time stopped, turned to Genny, and mouthed in mock silence, "Yes, of course," and resumed his descent.

Time initially thought the lack of a winter fire meant there was no homesteader or squatter. As he approached the shack, he noticed the thatched roof, with fresh boughs. Flat boards formed a makeshift porch, which faced in two directions, the path he was walking down, and another cut at an angle facing north but not uphill. Good defensive line of sight, he thought; then he froze.

Clothes on a line, drying. Small clothes. The smell of sweet waste, perhaps a compost, unseen, nearby. Then child-like voices and sounds. Very rapid, musical, could be one was whistling, or several at once. He could not discern what was being said, or how many children, but it was far from dangerous.

Two small girls, maybe five years old, thin and wan and identical, oblivious to the man with a rifle before them.

"Hello." Time tried to smile. Cloud's horse bayed a yawn from above on the slope.

The girls froze, wide-eyed. Their eyes spelled fear. One opened her mouth, and Time considered stopping her from screaming, but he was too far from the girls for it to appear like anything except an attack on them. The other girl put two fingers in her mouth, and spat a loud high shrill whistle that stopped the cold breeze and any life within hearing from breathing.

Then they clung to each other. The whistler took her twin's head and buried it in her own neck in protection.

"Hello, girls!" sang Genevieve.

Genny and Cloud began leading their horses down the slope to the shack, and the girls relaxed on seeing the women, but still held each other possessively.

A crash behind the shack, and a woman came running, followed by a boy not quite a teen with a crude bow and arrow, nocked. The girls flew to their mother, hugging her hips, and the matron reassured them by stroking their heads, though she never took her eyes off Time. She appeared unafraid, her gaunt and hard lined face and neck peeking through a blanket used as a winter coat. Her hips appeared heavy by the way the girls were holding her.

"Good afternoon, ma'am. We're travelers, going north."

"Put your weapon down, James," Genevieve sang. She had sensed a greater tension in the boy, and Time's rifle was too intimidating for casual conversation. By her assertion she implied a vague intimacy and control over the man, which would help explain her own pregnancy to the strangers.

Time complied. The boy then lowered his bow but kept the arrow nocked tight. Stepping in front of the woman and the girls, he took charge.

"We weren't expecting anyone." He looked at Cloud. "We haven't had anyone stop here in a long time, months. Before winter. The last two runaways were caught, and..." He looked at the matron.

"You are welcome here, if you're going north," she said simply. "But he'll put an arrow into you if you're a soldier come to steal. I'm Mrs. Carmody, and these are my children, Roger, and the girls are Margaret and Anne."

@@@

The first week was tenuous. Time and Cloud spent much of the hours after dark at their own fire, small but efficient, discussing little but how their lives had changed so radically, as if it was finally creeping into their consciousness like the winter cold.

They settled into a routine. Genny grew, as did the matron, Mrs. Carmody. Their pregnancies were close in time, but the resemblance ended there. Genny was happy to be off the horse, full of spirit, smiling and chatty. Mrs. Carmody was gloomy and moved woodenly, and only came out of her deep sadness when the two girls, her daughters, buried their faces in the folds of her heavy and shapeless clothing.

"I'm Roger. Roger Ballew." The boy challenged Time every minute they were together for the first few days. Time hid his smile, as the young man's seriousness would be easily bruised by a perceived mockery. Time enjoyed the spirit of the youngster, and pushed down thoughts of Roger becoming a soldier in this awful war.

"Is Mrs. Carmody your mother?"

"Yessir."

"But you're Ballew."

"'Cause I hate him. Father. I have only seen him every now and then, once in the fall and once in the spring every year. He hollers at me, frightens the girls, and keeps mother in the cabin all day and night. Last fall the little ones and me slept in the chapel…" He trailed off, looking slightly west, toward a heavily treed plateau, not fifty yards from the rock and clay and wood shack they called a cabin. Time saw this gesture, but sensed nothing unusual.

"Chapel?" Time thought it must be a small cave, or an odd tree with welcoming branches to sit upon. Those fifty or so yards west would bring them to what appeared to be a nearly vertical rock face covered in mosses and vines.

"Yessir. This way." The boy could barely contain his enthusiasm.

Roger stepped quickly, but slowed as the pines grew more dense, looking down. Time planted his feet on flat stones without disturbing the brush, following Roger's footfalls exactly without being told to do so. The dense vegetation in winter was cautionary. The stones were random but purposeful. As Time stepped on the first stone rising up, and the next, the trees and path changed. He clearly saw the narrow serpentine trail, lit with the deep black of stones intended for people to walk upon. After a few steps, Roger stopped, squinted, and plucked a berry amidst the chaos of wintry vegetation.

"They're so sweet here."

Time ducked low and followed the boy, and he felt the rise in the grade of the path, and could sense more than determine the plateau ahead, still hidden by dense brush and trees. The last steps were steep, and Roger ran to the top and disappeared over the edge.

Time puffed, stood upright in an open grotto, and whispered, "Oh."

In front of him was a stone slab held up by several knee-high boulders. The slab was smooth on top, jagged at the edges, and uneven to the ground. He marveled at how it could possibly have come to be there, smooth though rough-hewn, not level, not quite a table. It was an altar from the time before history, gray and blue and dirty white. Its opaqueness radiated with age.

To his right were many stones, headstones, forming a symmetrical graveyard, but facing the altar like a chapel. Several rows, perhaps six, with an aisle bisecting the otherwise perfect alignment of rocks of various shapes and height. Roger stood between the first two rows, his foot on one low stone. He grinned.

Time's eyes widened, and Roger's smile grew broadly.

"It's a chapel. Mother says these rocks are pews. I know it's a graveyard. I reckon there's over fifty people buried up here."

"Oh. Well, I'll be." Time looked to his left and saw several peaks high in the distance, through the clear winter sky. The mix of trees framed the view out and focused a person's gaze to the soft and sharp hills and ridges in the distance, the tops tinged in snow, one pushing the clouds out to encircle its trees in protection.

Yes, a chapel, Time thought. I could stay here all day and look at those hills, those peaks, the shimmering milky clouds.

"Mr. James?"

Time snapped out of his reflection, still smiling, and looked at a now very serious Roger.

"Yes, Roger. A chapel. It's beautiful."

"The last row? I just put in the stones. Nobody's buried there. I believe the first couple rows have many bodies, though. C' mere."

He walked purposefully to the last row that had high flat rocks jutting up.

"This is the best place to see the sunset. Mother doesn't come up here anymore, but the girls do, with me. Have a seat."

Time bent, knelt, and sat.

"This is a good seat, Roger." Time could only see the highest peaks, but the clouds were more prominent, looking through trees that formed the natural window above the altar.

"Splendid, son. Splendid."

Roger smiled again. "It's warmer here, too, for some reason. Even the rocks aren't cold, and the ground is dry. It's meant for us, given to us, I think." He leaned his head back and gazed over the altar, to the distance.

Time sighed, relaxed, and chuckled, "Roger Ballew, this is most peaceful. But you know," and he looked sideways at the boy, "all cemeteries are meant for us, sooner or later."

Roger tightened. "No. Yes. Not right now. This chapel is meant for mother, the girls, you, anyone. To set. To look."

Time interrupted. "To pray."

Roger hung his head. "I don't know how to pray, Mr. James."

"Sure you do, Roger. You talk to yourself, don't you?"

"Yessir."

"Then you can pray."

"Why am I praying?"

"Well, uh, to ask for things."

"You mean for food? And shoes? I could use shoes."

"No. Yes. Well, I think it's better to pray for others, not for things. Pray for your mother, and your little sisters. Prayer for others is very very powerful, Roger."

Roger cocked his head, keeping his gaze on the peaks as the clouds parted enough for the sun to poke through.

"Do you pray for me?"

"Yes. Well, I can. Yes. I will."

Roger's tongue worked quickly over his lips.

"Who do you pray to?"

"God. Roger let's do this one prayer I know. Repeat after me. Our Father..."

After they finished, Time wanted to explain it. The orphans were still raw in the front of his mind, and he knew that no matter how he could have trained them, they were all only borrowing moments under the cold winter sun. Time realized now that he could have done better by talking to the boy soldiers about faith. His own tenuous grip on it should not have barred him from trying to be a better leader, one of the human spirit. He would do so with this boy, Roger.

"Roger, this is the most important prayer you can say. You are praying for everyone, not just yourself. You acknowledge God's power, and you thank Him for all the abundance life offers. But the biggest part of this prayer is about forgiveness. Lastly we ask that we avoid sin and evil avoids us. It's about all of us, under His watchful eye." Time could tell by the boy's expression that he wasn't quite listening, and had understood little of it.

"Yes, but why? I know He is God and all, but... if I pray and bad things happen, then God doesn't like me. And I try my best, Mr. James, I truly do!" His agitation was acute, and it tore at Time to see it.

"It's not easy, Roger. God made everything, but He doesn't make everything happen. I think He gave us life to do good things. Righteous things. But bad things happen... not because of God, but because men are weak, or stupid, or cowards, or greedy, or..."

"Soldiers," Roger whispered.

Time turned slightly to face Roger, whose eyes were brimming.

"I know you're a soldier. I heard Genny and Cloud talking."

"I was a soldier, son. Not anymore." Time's eyes now burned. He saw the faces of Adam and Goff and Fish and all of them as he looked at Roger's cowlick.

"The man with the red beard isn't a soldier."

"What man?"

"He was here in the fall. Says he's mother's 'comlaw husband'. He laughed about it. Mother is jittery around him."

"Is he..."

"I don't think so."

Time sat straight. "You'll not have to worry about him as long as I am here. You'll be ready when I'm gone, too. I will make sure of that."

Roger slipped to his knees and the words came in a rush.

"I know. I'm gonna show you what I've done, done to get ready for him next time. But you can't tell the women yet."

The first few rows were graves, neat but narrow, less than five or six feet separating them head to toe. Side by side there was no gap. The last two rows had been placed there by the boy.

"I'm gonna start selling the graves. For money."

"You have a lot of people dying up here?"

"No, nobody yet, but we've gotten travelers, like you and Cloud, and they might want to buy a grave now. Be ready, of a sort."

"How many travelers over the years?" Time didn't want to dampen Roger's enthusiasm.

"Well, every spring there's somebody. Two and three at a time, like you, moving slaves up north, secret-like. Only the one bad man last fall, and the spring before that, but everyone else real polite and friendly and generous. See?" He held up a substantial steel knife. "This knife is razor sharp. I can clean a squirrel or 'coon in nothing at all long's I keep it sharp."

"Any of these travelers die?"

"No. But everybody dies, right?"

"Usually healthy people don't buy their own grave when they're travelling, I think."

Roger thought about that. "I 'spect you might be right. But..."

"But what?"

Roger lowered his voice, conspiratorially. "I had a dream I would be digging up here. So I started to dig."

Roger stepped to the last row.

"Look here." Roger crouched, sank his clawed fingers into the earth near the first stone of the last row and pulled toward himself while crab-walking backwards. The deep green unbroken thicket of grass and moss peeled away from the black earth. After four stone widths, about eight feet, as Roger efficiently rolled the sod, he stopped.

A hole two feet wide, less than two feet deep, just a square slit under the earth.

Roger beamed. "It's a beaut, isn't it?"

Time again smiled, trying to avoid a cynical tone.

"That's not how a grave is dug, Roger."

"I know that." Roger snorted crossly. "This hole is gonna hide us when a bad sort comes."

Time clapped his hands together. "Of course! You can get two or three people in there, packed tight."

"Or a mother and her three children!"

"You done good, Roger. I never saw the seam of the hole..."

"Watch. I'll get in." Roger climbed in the hole, and effortlessly pulled the rolled sod over himself. In the light Time could see the outline, but only because he knew where to look. An interloper would not look too closely at graves, even if he could find this rock chapel. Someone who had been here wouldn't find the hide-hide.

Roger, still under the sod, pushed a corner out and peered at Time.

"I can see you smiling through the grass, Roger, come on out." The woman and the three children would fit there but it would be tight, he thought, no room for fidgeting. Roger stood with his hands on his hips.

As if reading Time's mind, Roger said, "I think I can make it deeper or wider."

"Maybe. But you don't want to invite ground water or critters. Go real deep, or leave it as it is. Lord willing, you won't need it."

Roger looked pensive, a sad face on the boy. "Maybe we should pray real hard about this."

Time respected the youngster's commitment to his family's security. But he knew that even the strongest conviction could be fatal if not balanced with wisdom.

"Roger."

"Yessir?"

"When we rode up last week, you didn't hear us until we were close. What makes you think you'll have enough time to get up here, together, and get in the hole quietly? What if you don't know the danger until it exposes its intent?"

"And then it's too late." A statement by Roger, not a challenge, not a question. His bony shoulders sank, his chin collapsed in resignation. He brightened quickly. "But we do have a crawlspace under mother's bed, out the back-like. It could work."

"Good job, Roger. We can think this through. Together. We'll have to show the girls soon enough. We can do a drill."

"Now I have something to pray for, Mr. James."

@@@

It took a week before Mrs. Carmody could have everyone sit at one time for meals. That sort of civilized manner had not been what the small family was used to, but the woman thought that guests are guests and they would try to do things correctly.

Time was entertaining throughout the modest meal, and Cloud was most complimentary of what little food was available, and the effort put forth. The two of them provided almost all the conversation, as the home was acute in its poverty.

"I'm glad you're here, Miss Cloud. You're a thinker. Your book reading has done you a great service. Perhaps you can read to the children. We'll be safer because of it." Time was ready to give Cloud the job of talking to the family.

Cloud, embarrassed, tried to hide her skepticism. "When things are at their darkest, we'll need someone who can conjugate verbs."

"Huh?" Mrs. Carmody thought she heard something obscene.

"I've never heard a lady talk like that," piped in Roger.

Time smiled. "That's no lady, son. That's an education. A good one, too."

Roger shrugged, stood, and said to no one, "'Bout time I went to work." He walked out the door with a horse brush.

"I'll go, too. I am feeling most full and would like to stand. May I be excused, Mrs. Carmody?" Genny's sweetness had smitten everyone, especially Mrs. Carmody.

"Of course, my dear. Roger is sensitive. When he doesn't understand things he just jumps right up, and, well, he just needs some attention, is all."

"I'll show him how to brush the horses, if they're not sleeping." Genny followed Roger out.

Cloud knew her cue. "Mrs. Carmody, I would like to read to your daughters. May I?"

The matron sniffed. "I suppose that would be fine."

Time interjected, as the girls whistled and peeped approval, "I am very much looking forward to this, Miss Cloud. Thank you."

@@@

Cloud exercised the horses daily during the hardness of winter, while Time and Roger hunted, foraged, and generally kept away from the women. Genny fussed over the girls, trying to coax words from them, usually only receiving responses in whistles and peeps.

Mrs. Carmody tried to explain to Genny. "I know they can speak, because they can hear me talk. I've never whistled or what-have-you to them, or anyone, for that matter. Margaret whistles. Anne peeps. It might be the only way to tell them apart."

The two girls, not quite five years old, were identical right down to the dirt in their fingernails. Matted flaxen hair, blue eyes, small even teeth flanked by dimples that were evident without the encouragement of a smile, deep and piercing while laughing or pouting. Genevieve thought they were both painfully adorable, but noted that the resemblance to their mother ended with the pale blue eyes.

"What do they say to you?"

"Momma."

Genny smiled. "That's all?"

"Well, no, but it's been a long time since they've tried actual sentences. Whistles and peeps. They understand each other well enough, that's for certain."

"Why doesn't your son talk to them?"

"Oh, he does, in his way. He whistles and peeps, too, thinks he knows how they listen. The girls laugh at him, sweetly, like he was saying something foreign and embarrassing. He laughs with them." She looked away. "It's the only time he laughs, my dear." And she looked at her feet. "He's a serious young man. Frets for us. Protective."

"But he's only a boy, so small."

"He's got a big heart, Genevieve. Roger has big plans. Wants to sell graves up at the rock chapel and build a hostel for travelers."

They settled into silence, taking the scraps of fabric, doubling them over, and rough cross-stitching it together. It was brutal hard-fingered work. The thread was a hemp twine, the needles curved and dull. Mrs. Carmody had explained the endless bed sheet and blankets would be necessary if the wood ran out, or the thatched timber roof failed. They kept at it, hour after hour. Genny was content, as travel was most painful for her at this stage. She enjoyed talking about the sensations inside her, and Mrs. Carmody made small endearments of understanding and support. The endless blankets had no real purpose than to give them purpose, as they both awaited the natural course of their lives in the haven of warmth of an uneven earthen home.

@@@

Time and Cloud communicated silently throughout the day, in an understanding that the family's poverty was something that contributed to the little girls' lack of communication skills. Neither would encourage the girls to do anything but talk, and Time mostly ignored them when they whistled and peeped themselves silly. One unusually warm spring day Genny was playing with the girls, who were both sensitive to Genny's condition and bursting with energy and joy. Time, after hearing one too many "peeps" from Anne, started to mimic her, and "peeped" to Cloud who was nearby. Since Cloud was a poor whistler, they both began laughing at the girls and the entire situation at hand.

The girls knew they were being mocked, and ran away, sulking with hooded eyes, and Genny found herself breathing from exertion and standing in front of the two adults, the magic of her playtime with the little girls broken.

"It's not that complicated. She can't whistle," said Genevieve, hands on growing hips, looking at Time and Cloud with a measure of admonition.

Time and Cloud stole glances. They had presumed a self-righteousness and protectiveness of Genny, thinking she was intelligent but remarkably naive. The clarity of Genny's observation weighed upon both the soldier and the would-be slave. It's that kind of assumption that could get us all killed someday, thought Time. He vowed to be more observant.

Time and Cloud avoided casual conversation with each other after that. Cloud fussed over Genny more than ever as each day brought a new revelation for the pregnant girl, and Time devoted the waking hours to Roger when they weren't exercising the horses and finding grass to feed them. The separation and intimacy in so small a homestead fit the family dynamic.

@@@

They stayed for a couple months before and through the spring thaw. Both Mrs. Carmody and Genevieve grew heavy with child, and the unnaturally warm winter spat into a cold and icy April. Time now spent most of his hours keeping the horses warm and fed and exercised, while Roger did small tasks to assist, they both spending many sunsets at the rock chapel. Cloud kept the girls occupied inside the shack, plugging holes in the ceiling and walls, stemming the tide of insects and rodents in their search for food. Every comfort of the small house was created and tenderly given to Mrs. Carmody and Genny by all.

The rumble of thunder drifted down the slope and seemed to seek and stop at the house late one night after a two day break of sunshine and thawing trees and growth. The hut concussed, and the sudden severity made everyone cling to each other, though Time grabbed his rifle and sat with his back to the door, as if his armed presence could stay the spring storm. The lightning made the earthen hut look like day, even when shuttered completely from the outside, exposing its numerous imperfections. The boomboomboom grew louder and angrier, then a ringing silence, and both women's water broke at almost the same instant, the light and crash of thunder happening on top of each other and the rain coming in a torrent.

The girls clung to each other in desperation and fear. Roger calmly lit and relit candles. Cloud moved from one shaken woman to the other, Genny fighting hysteria, Mrs. Carmody in great pain but stoic. Now Time faced the door, at port arms.

"I need your help, James Time. I need your help." Cloud said evenly, plainly, unsure if he heard her urgency under the words.

His chest heaved. Genny screeched and her legs flew out. Cloud knew she would have to tend to both women without ever having done this before, or even witnessing it. She imagined it was not unlike a single horse birth she had witnessed years before. She had never seen a more violent unbidden act.

Mrs. Carmody whispered, "Cloud, have her set up, push something behind her back, knees up, girl." She had the authority of weary experience, and as she spoke to Cloud she mimicked her own commands.

"Mother, what do I do?" Roger was more concerned than frightened, and glanced sidelong at the immobile Time.

"Nothing, uh, uh, dear. Nothing."

Mrs. Carmody continued to spit and hiss and whisper commands. Genny's cries consumed the air in the hut, and Roger fussed about without doing anything, occasionally trying to soothe his sisters, who blinked at him and otherwise ignored the entreaty. Cloud whispered in soft bird coos to Genny, and Whistle and Peep stayed silent, staring from one agonized pregnant woman to the other.

Time continued to face the door, eyes clamped shut, oblivious to his surroundings, an inert focus of detachment. I cannot help them, he thought in pain, so I will not try.

Genny screamed twice, Mrs. Carmody and Cloud at the ready, and the child came into the flickering light. The baby coughed and gulped air, and Cloud exclaimed, *"It's a girl!"* franticly trying to hold the little one without dropping her. Whistle and Peep were silent in awe. Time whipped his head around to look.

Mrs. Carmody let out a bellow of air, and then she held her blue child in her hands, her own head slumped, wet, and dazed.

@@@

When the young die, the echoes of their short lives get louder as our vision of their light fades, our brief encounters with them now epoch through the ordinary passage of time. The Carmody child never made a sound, but Time heard its birth, saw its death, and would be forever frozen thinking of the life the boy could have had.

@@@

The thunder became distant and rumbled harmlessly, competing with the steady drum of rain on the thatched wooden roof. The room was warm and the air thick. The girls slept with their heads on Mrs. Carmody's thighs, whose own head was thrown back in exhaustion, her mouth wide, breathing loudly and deeply.

The baby gurgled and fussed in Cloud's arms, alert and restless. Genevieve and Cloud were beaming, relieved, proud, and overwhelmed.

Roger sat sleeping at Time's feet, Time still standing facing the door nearly an hour after the births. Head bent and crown pressed to the wood, he was imitating sleep, but still acutely alert.

One night without sleep in a timeless hell, Time thought, but better than being frozen in helpless fear.

Yet he froze, nakedly and cowardly, having been in this mental place before, long ago, and knowing the outcome would not be good. Too much then, too much now. He had been frozen, and could not act when required to do something, anything, even if just to witness. He suppressed a sob of self-loathing.

"Sergeant Time." Cloud may have said his name only once, or a hundred times. They were the first words he heard and understood in hours.

"Yes. Yes, Cloud."

"I thought you might be awake." She handed the twitching newborn to Genny, who pulled the babe tight to her chest. Standing, Cloud approached the immobile man, and rested her hand on the small of his back.

"We need you now."

"Yes." A cough, dry and weak.

"Mrs. Carmody's child is dead. You and Roger need to bury it at first light."

"Dead?" Time already knew it, but the confirmation was necessary.

"Yes. Before the birth, I think. Do it as soon as the rain stops. Please bundle the child tightly. Mrs. Carmody has already said her good-byes and doesn't want the girls upset anymore." Cloud looked at the sleeping figure of the sturdy woman.

"I hear a baby."

"Genevieve had a girl. She's perfect. Not a hair on her head and looks just like her. Perfect."

Time couldn't help but smile, and wanted to turn to face Cloud, but the comfort of the small woman's hand on his back was the only genuinely selfless touch he had felt in years. He wished it forever and just as quickly Cloud removed it.

Time turned and faced her.

"Lord, Sergeant Time, you look worse than either woman. Get some water. Rest, now." Cloud moved back to Genny, lay close, and closed her eyes. Time drank cleanly from the ladle, replaced it smoothly and without sound. He gazed upon Genny and her child, the perfect baby girl.

"I'll name her Jesse," Genny said sweetly, without looking up at Time.

"Ah. Wisdom and understanding, I believe."

"Yes, Sergeant Time. That's what I have been thinking all these months. I don't need to know why, why I'm now a mother, why Adam and Goff are dead, why mother and father had passed what seems like so long ago." She sighed.

"Jesse is a handsome name for a girl, Genny."

The baby attached herself to Genevieve, and mother and child both closed their eyes.

Two candle flames were nearly out. Roger must have cut the oil lamp earlier, thought Time. The rain stopped in a whisper. Time then lay down on the floor next to Roger, and slept.

Time dreamt, conscious of sleep, thinking that one good night's rest, one peaceful night for all, was a bountiful wealth of good for their souls, a too brief relief from life's pain.

The silence soon after in the early morning light was gently pushed aside by the rustling of clothes and deliberate action by the girls to try not to upset the others nearby, a polite intention that rapidly became impractical, then impossible.

Whistle and Peep started their morning ritual, which grew in tempo and pitch as they unwrapped their dead sibling, having dreamt of a miracle.

"No, no, no, girls, it's time we said goodbye." Mrs. Carmody was firm but soothing, and did not want to share her ache.

"Roger. Roger."

"Yes, mum."

Cloud was awake, yet kept silent. She wanted to stay with Genny and the new baby, but was torn to go with Time and Roger to say a prayer, one prayer, as the stillborn infant was laid to rest.

"Genny, Cloud, I'm going to bury Mrs. Carmody's baby, now." The natural timber in Time's voice had not yet returned.

"Yes, yes, I'm fine, sergeant, you go," Genny reassured him.

The girls had stopped making their noises, and looked longingly at Genny's sleeping baby in wonder. They each kept one hand on their mother, a subtle and unconscious act of both possession and division, torn between their mother's comfort to them, and the curiosity of a newborn. Mrs. Carmody knew and smiled, and spoke softly to her daughters.

"Girls, wash your hands first. Stoke the fire and heat water, but have clean hands. Then go see Genny's baby."

"Her name is Jesse," Genny whispered.

"A lovely name, Genevieve, lovely."

Time stepped to the matron, knelt, and was handed the tight motionless bundle. Roger and Cloud were already by his side.

"Is this your wish, Mrs. Carmody?" More a statement than a question, from Time.

"Yes. Thank you."

Roger knelt by his mother, cradled her shoulder, and kissed her forehead. The girls looked on open-mouthed. Mrs. Carmody patted her son's arm, closed her eyes, and said, "Go."

Time, Cloud and Roger opened the door and stepped into a cool misty emerging sun. The girls began daybreak rituals. Just another morning.

@@@

Weeks passed, and as the sky brightened the earth warmed the hut and the grotto. The hobbled horses were now used to the near sounds of the forest, comfortable with young human voices and their own silent habits. They rarely moved unless Time coaxed them, one at a time, on an hour's daily walk or trot on the hillside at midday. As long as the beasts had each other, they were content in repose.

After four straight days of good cloudless sunshine, Time was restless to get moving.

"We should take advantage that the spring rain is done."

No one else wanted to leave. The girls were happy, Roger productive, and Genny was strong, though she struggled to nurse the baby Jesse. Mrs. Carmody helped suckle the baby on occasion and Jesse grew measurably under her feeding. Cloud's only remaining personal treasure, a torn and incomplete copy of Dickens' *Bleak House*, was read in bursts nightly to all, though the third reading may have been too much for Time's patience.

"We'll have visitors soon enough. We don't know who." He noted Mrs. Carmody and Roger exchanged a conspiratorial glance. "Remember, I'm a deserter. We need to move."

The children ignored him, hiding their fear in their games. Mrs. Carmody went back to sewing. Cloud, Roger, and Time walked outside and approached the horses.

"Roger, get some water, please, I'd like to brush the horse."

"There's water in the bucket, Cloud, why not..."

She cut him off, ungently. "Get it now."

Roger darted away, as Time apprised Cloud with a raised eyebrow.

"Well?"

"We should leave in a day or two. We need to pack the horses tightly, of course. And we need to take the children."

Time was dumbstruck. After Jesse's birth, Cloud hadn't spoken to the children unless necessary, as she doted on Genny and the baby to a fault. He knew she couldn't abide the whistles and peeps any more than he could, and maybe less. Roger's dour nature toward her was often disrespectful and sometimes unpleasant.

"No, Cloud. We need to move, and there's too many for three horses. We need flexibility, not a burden. The baby is anchor enough."

Cloud nodded. "You're right, but..."

"But what?"

"We'll stay, you go."

"Are you daft? You can't stay here!"

The horses neighed and scuffed.

"We can and we will. Leave two horses, and one weapon, the rifle. When the summer heat is up, and we've collected a visitor or two, we'll move north with them."

Time could hear the lack of confidence in Cloud's voice. Not from her plan, but in his inability to guide them safely north. Since the birth of Jesse, she trusted him less. And somewhere deep inside he wanted to travel alone.

"I can get us safely to Pennsylvania, Cloud. I can reckon north as good as anyone."

"Not as good as those who have been doing it through here each season. Besides, your presence with us is a liability. The railroad will be our guide and salvation."

"So it's not just about the Carmody's, the children."

"No it is not. It is only about Genevieve and Jesse. Only them. We don't count, James Time, and you know it."

The horses stopped moving as Cloud stroked the neck of the brown mare, the largest of the group. She looked intently into the horse's mane. Time wanted to reassure her, but could not. His last action in the face of crisis was terribly inadequate.

"I'll think about it, Cloud. But I'm not convinced. I will tell you my thoughts in the morning."

@@@

Cloud began reading her book aloud, again, after the evening meal of rabbit and dried berries. Mrs. Carmody stated plainly that unless there was a visitor soon, their supplies of staples would be gone. They were living on wild bitter berries and mushrooms, rabbits and birds, and the stripped carcass of a buck whose meat had toughened into bands of tough jerky.

The girls mouthed words in imitation of Cloud in the flickering light as she read aloud. Mrs. Carmody and Genny and Roger all smiled silently. Time shook his head, stood, stretched, and reached for the door just as all the horses neighed intently, not fiercely, but with a startled urgency that froze everyone.

Roger whispered, "Follow mother, now. We'll use the crawlspace like we done before."

The drill to the rock chapel hide-hole had been performed grudgingly twice that month, in daylight. The last shimmer of sun had left long before. Mrs. Carmody moved the raised bed, pulled the two planks that covered the escape hole, and crawled into it. The girls followed closely, then Cloud holding Jesse, then Genny and Roger, who whispered to Time.

"Are you coming?"

"Yes. Just listen." A pause. Time wanted to make sure there was an interloper, or worse, a bear.

The horses neighed again, louder. A traveler at night in unfamiliar territory would hail the light from the hut if seeking shelter. But a silent familiarity with the terrain meant only one thing, and it was not of good intent. Danger was near.

"Damn." Time sat in the hole and replaced the bed. Cradling his rifle, he crawled on his elbows and knees and made for the steps.

The girls and Mrs. Carmody knew where the flat stone steps were once they reached the base of the hill under the chapel. The reflection of the steps glimmered and disappeared, but the girls' confidence and sure-footed touch emboldened Cloud. Roger kept a hand on Genny's elbow, and she kept the fingertips of her right hand on the small of Cloud's back, as if to stay connected to both her friend and her baby.

Walking quickly and gingerly, they crept into the chapel, sped past the uneven altar, down the aisle bisecting the headstones, and fell to their knees at the last row. Roger began to pull back the turf, when a crash was heard at the hut below.

"Oh, no!" Whistle yelped.

Peep hushed her, "Quiet, Margaret!"

Mrs. Carmody lay in the hole, just as was drilled, and the girls folded themselves around her. Cloud gestured with her head for Genny to lay down, head to toe with Mrs. Carmody, then laid the baby in Genny's arms. Cloud darted her head from side to side, unsure if she would fit, and looked up startlingly just as Time approached.

"Get in."

Roger then rolled the turf carpet over the women. He and Time knelt by the hole, Roger smoothing the grass.

Time put his mouth to Roger's ear. "Follow me."

They moved to the highest rear stones, just a few feet from where the girls lay. They waited, believing and hoping the interloper might just stay where the hut was, where the warm embers of a dying fire beckoned, and horses easy for the taking. Maybe he was a friendly sort.

Another sudden crash, and an explosion of curses came from the hut below. An angry man.

Roger whispered to Time. "I'm praying, Sergeant James, I am. Praying he'll leave. I think it's that man with the red beard."

Time knew of this man, this Redbeard, the man who kept Mrs. Carmody as hostage last fall and the spring before while the children had to fend for themselves, the one who frightened Roger. Time had heard of his reputation as an outlaw who was gruesome and cruel, and thought it just nonsense and campfire legend. Now his imagination was on fire. He also knew that such cowards of violence did not always travel alone, and that they might now be outmanned, outgunned, and out of luck.

Time whispered to Roger, "He or they will be up here soon, I suspect. Does he know of this hole?"

"No."

"The chapel?"

"Yes."

"Well, son, he might smell us, or hear the baby. Look, we have to be ready. You may need to distract him and then I'll shoot him with my pistol. Take the rifle, and use only as a last resort, if I'm dead, okay? On my command, Roger, mine alone."

Roger was wild-eyed with fear and determination, the conflicting orders making perfect sense in his head.

Another short but loud crash of discarded metal, and then the unmistakable rustle of brush being moved from the foot of the steps.

They could feel the presence of the man in the open night air of the chapel before they could see or hear him. The heavy footfalls and deep raspy breathing played over the normal night sounds.

Time gestured to Roger to stand and run away from the aisle, into the woods, and Time would shoot the interloper; Time was pointing and moving his eyes, just black and white orbs to Roger, Roger nodding and bracing himself against the heavy stone.

It was too dark to see any shadows in the partial moon and starlight. The crack of small tinder under the man's boots was clear in signaling his proximity. Ten feet, maybe five feet away.

Roger nodded his readiness.

Time, his right arm numb from the awkward crouch, dropped his pistol. "Damn."

Roger launched himself not to the trees, but into the aisle, right at the feet of the man. Roger raised the rifle awkwardly, firing once, missing the massive form, who levelled his own long gun within inches of the boy's forehead.

"Bad move, little man."

Time stood, stepped once, and plunged his cutting knife under the man's ribcage, center, and pushed up, turning the handle.

The man bellowed and stopped, and his rifle roared, the single round ricocheting and breaking off a head-stone and burying itself in pieces into the ground.

The man's eyes were brown and wide, his mouth an odd grimace surrounding imperfect teeth. Staring at Time, he rasped his last breath, and fell backwards still clutching his weapon as Time withdrew his own knife from the man's chest. The interloper's head struck stone, and his discharged rifle hit another at the trigger mech-anism and the weapon bent and cracked.

The man had a short stubble of beard. Black.

"Roger! You, why?"

"You dropped your gun! You dropped it!"

Muffled cries of shock came from under the turf a few feet away.

Roger bolted to the hide-hole as Time surveyed the rock chapel. The man he killed was probably alone, or Time would have heard someone react to the two shots, though he wanted to be sure. Roger scrambled, peeled back the turf and reached out to the women, but no one moved as yet. He thought Genny's frock was light blue, not the dark color he saw now.

"Oh, no."

Cloud grabbed Jesse from Genny's arms, then began shaking her friend with her other arm.

"Genny, Gen, Gen... no, no, no..."

"Hush, quiet, now. We're not safe yet."

"No no no no..."

Time scanned the area again. Nothing. No noises of pursuit or flight from the grotto. The man had been alone, and was swarthy and dark featured, certainly young, and no red beard.

No. No. No. No.

Whistle and Peep chirped idiotically, frightened and overwhelmed while Mrs. Carmody ran her hands over them, checking for wounds.

No. No.

"Must have glanced off the stone, from the shot, the second one."

Roger was excited, "It wasn't me! I shot at him, up!"

"No, Roger, it wasn't you. He did it. As he was dying. After I stabbed him."

Time knelt at Genevieve's side, she still in the hole, now alone. Cloud clutched the baby and heaved repeatedly in disbelief. Roger knelt at Time's side, looked at his mother and sisters, and shook his head to them, no no no.

Time found the wound at Gen's neck, deep, long, and unquestionably fatal. She was already gone.

"Oh, dear God, no." Time closed Genny's eyes. He turned his attention to the dead man not ten feet away, grabbing Roger's collar in the same move.

"You know this man?"

Roger looked intently at the fallen open-mouthed figure, as if there might be some recognition, some reason this man was dead. He slowly shook his head, no.

"Oh, damn all."

"This is a chapel, Mr. Time."

They all stared at Margaret, the whistler, and Cloud cried heavily and squeezed baby Jesse to her chest.

@@@

In the morning it was decided to bury Genevieve right where she died. Time said the Our Father three times. They all clutched dirt and dropped the cold clots onto her inert and soiled form, calm in repose after Peep crossed Gen's hands. Roger covered the grave with sticks and scrub and stones large and small. The women then walked back to the hut.

"We leave in an hour," Time said, loud enough for all to hear, but unacknowledged by anyone.

Time and Roger dug a shallow grave near the altar, where the dirt was loose. Time stripped off the interloper's boots, taking the suspenders, knife and canteen. The useless rifle was buried with him. The man had no identifier and was unknown to the Carmody's.

And the stranger left them an enormous gift, a mule laden with grain, oats, salt pork, coffee, hardtack, sugar and salt, all army issue, and all stolen and disguised for black market sale. Time knew that if the man wasn't followed directly he might well be soon, so they must leave immediately. He could have been a spy or just a thief with an idea for profit or to buy his passage north through bribes.

It was also Time's chance for a clean break and he knew he had to act now, while everyone was still numb from Genny's death. He cursed his selfishness, and looked up as the early morning clouds began to drift by overhead. He envied the clouds, their constant movement, sometimes thin, sometimes muscular, often stacked high, then opaque and veiled. Storms were created when clouds conflicted, he thought, dark and complicated one moment, invisible another. Clouds went where and when they took themselves, accountable to nature, completing the mood of the day, often entertaining and begging him to look up to an image of the majesty and fleeting breath of life.

"Come inside, Mr. Time. We must eat before we leave," called Mrs. Carmody.

"You are a rock, woman. Thank you." Time could not meet her eye as he walked past her into the hut.

The others sat facing each other around the slat table. All fit easily now, no one saying the obvious, that Genny's absence gave them more space to sit. Time sat, coughed, and began to explain the urgency of the need to leave right away. The baby started to squirm in Cloud's arms, fussing and hungry, and cried seemingly for the first time since she had been born.

Mrs. Carmody spoke soothingly. "Give her to me." The girls looked at the baby with envy. Since their mother's milk was abundant, they had enjoyed nursing from her for almost a month.

Mrs. Carmody cradled the child to her, who eagerly nuzzled and fed. The girls stared open-mouthed at their mother, who cooed sweetly about how big they were and now the baby Jesse can only have milk, which elicited two whistles and a peep.

The air in the room became heavy and small sounds thudded like drums. Cloud looked stricken, eyes wide, and Roger touched her arm. His exhaustion was acute.

"Do you need to sleep, Cloud?" Roger asked.

"We can't sleep right yet, Roger. We have to pack up and go. Now." Time was paternal but firm.

Cloud stood. "I'll have the horses ready right away." She walked out of the hut before she was finished talking. Time walked out after her. Roger and the girls rested their heads on the table, and each fell into an uncomfortable slumber of sheer exhaustion, the only sound in the hut the soft feeding of the orphan on a stranger's breast.

Within the hour Time had checked and re-checked the mule's packing and took a detailed mental inventory of the provisions. There was enough for all of them for a month or more, he thought, if we aren't waylaid first.

Time called out. "We don't need anything but blankets, Mrs. Carmody. There is plenty here for all of us on the trail, for a long time. The only thing we'll need is wood."

Mrs. Carmody hummed, walking with the baby around the cave-like hut, viewing the surroundings with a mix of regret and revulsion. Her bond with the infant was nearly complete, and Jesse was content.

"Of course, Mr. Time."

The girls were running and acting out, whistling and whispering in monosyllabic peeps.

Cloud returned from one last trip to the rock chapel, her third in the last hour, her face drawn, her eyes heavily lidded. Her acceptance of Genny's fate was nearly complete.

Roger stood in front of Time, and sharply saluted.

Time offered a tight smile. "Private Roger Ballew, we'll be doubling up on the horses." To all he said, "I do not want to ride the mule. Our provisions are too valuable and I don't know how he'll react. There's no saddle so I can't determine if it's worth the risk."

"The horses are ready," Cloud said, flatly.

"Cloud, you and Roger take the lead. Mrs. Carmody will go second with the child, and..." Cloud stiffened, and all eyes watched her. She made a fist, and struck her own hip, but said nothing.

Her sharp resignation said it all. She wanted the baby Jesse, her sister's baby, but it would be impractical. In the one second of painful recognition, her shoulders slumped, and Cloud relented.

"Come, Roger." She walked to her mare.

"And you girls will ride with me!" Time spread his arms wide.

"Good!" Whistles and peeps.

"None of that, mind you, not anymore. You are young ladies now. We are on the move, and we can't be sounding like a circus."

"Mr. Time!" Mrs. Carmody flashed with mild anger, nearly coming out of her reverie.

"It's Sergeant Time, Ma'am. Now get saddled."

Roger helped his mother sit straight on Gen's horse, and then he sat on the high rump of Cloud's mare. Time reached to the outstretched arms of the twin girls, who each said a polite thank you, one in front of him, one behind.

It will be a slow journey, he thought, but we must move now. "Go ahead, Cloud."

Each looked sadly at the rise up the stone slope leading to the rock chapel. Cloud sighed heavily, and the girls clutched at Time. The horses began forward as one. Although the pace was careful and each step measured, the press to move north remained steady, the weather in favor during the day. Large tapestry quilts would be their tent cover at night, and if not for Time's anxiety over capture the trip had all the marking of an extended family outing.

10

The Run

Twenty miles a day. The strength of the horses and fresh water and new grass for their sustenance were the only limits to speed. A week passed uneventfully, mostly in silence and grief.

"Our pace is good," said Time to no one. "The denser the brush, now that spring is helping, the better we'll be."

"Do you think the Underground they speak of uses this trail?" Cloud's concern over having no freeman's papers while still skirting Virginia mounted with each day.

"Let's hope the successful ones," said Time, absently.

"I haven't seen any horse droppings ahead of us, Cloud, so I think that no one uses these woods, at least not recently," Roger offered.

Each day warmed a little more, and less energy was wasted in trying to fight the chill. The nights were cold, mostly dry, and they stayed close together. Time slept little.

"Can we stop for a moment?" Mrs. Carmody asked for relief. "Cloud, she's fed, would you hold her?"

Cloud eagerly dismounted and moved quickly to the woman, taking the child Jesse before the matron could dismount.

The horses were always at ease when Cloud was near them.

"I have to pee, too, please," Margaret said, sheepishly.

"Me, too! Me, too!" Squealed Anne, and Time swung one girl, then the other, down from his horse, and then dismounted himself.

The girls scurried close by, modesty being a luxury long abandoned by them. Mrs. Carmody's head could be clearly seen cresting over the bushes not twenty feet away. Time and Roger relieved themselves not far from the rear of the trailing mule, as Cloud tended to Jesse.

"Roger, help me give the horses a quick brush," then louder, "We move in a few minutes, ladies, stretch and work your legs."

@@@

"Why do you people hate each other so?" Cloud hissed at Time when they were alone at the campfire after the others had gone to rest for the night.

They had avoided speaking to each other since Genny's death. Cloud could barely contain her fury and disgust with Time, and rather than fight it, he avoided her.

"Who is we? We don't hate each other. Who am I supposed to hate?" He could not understand this complicated strong-willed woman.

"People. *Your* people. This war. This *noble* cause." Cloud's venom was rushing forth.

"Nonsense. Stop it. I do not hate anybody." Time was exhausted.

"Of course you do. You kill each other for words."

"Words?"

"Yes! States' rights! Or to preserve a Union! Or to free men. And now you hate us, too!"

"Nonsense, Cloud. We don't hate you, we..."

"Pity us."

"Yes. No. But, you hate us, too!"

"No. We don't trust you. We never will."

"Malarkey. It's just hate, is all."

"I don't hate my family, the Moases, Miss Genny... or you. But I can't completely trust you."

"Why is that? Can't you accept me as a man, on what I do?"

"That can change, and..."

"Again, nonsense. Those boys died for you and Genny and your comfort. You should respect that."

"I do, God knows I do. But even they never looked past my skin. By law I am property."

"Your brothers, Adam and Goff, always treated you like a sister, not a slave. They respected you. Most of those other soldiers never owned a slave, and never would."

"Oh, yes, yes, I know. The boys hated no one, probably not even the enemy."

"I think you do hate us, for all of this." Time was angered by her attitude.

"No, not you, Sergeant Time. I do not hate you. And I have to trust you, I have no other recourse."

"And the boys who died. They proved and earned your trust, too, I pray, having taken it to a cold, shallow grave."

Cloud became enraged. "That was never my, our, intent. *Your* hatred, your inability to see us as people through our lifetimes, has brought us here, sir, not *our* hate. *Your* hate. Of each other. Of mankind."

"I cannot fathom your depth, Cloud. You believe what you believe, but you are wrong. We don't hate you. We don't hate each other. This is all about money, and power."

"My point precisely, Sergeant Time. All of you. You hate people. You love money and power."

"I do not!"

"No, you probably don't. But the people who put all this in motion, who direct your armies, who make high handed speeches and seek high handed office... they hate people."

@@@

The original panic of flight stepped downwards to a vigilant walk. Most of the days passed with nothing but an occasional horse's snort or a sneeze from Roger, who managed to frighten everyone with the abrupt velocity of his discharges.

"Hay fever," he would say. "Sorry."

Time was not amused at first, but his sense of stealth and security waned with each hour of the day.

"That boy will lose an eye if he keeps sneezing like that."

Roger made one attempt to suppress it, which only caused his right eye to go bloodshot for the rest of the day. After that, he would jam two knuckles up his nose to stop the potential threat.

Day after day, the same routine, blessed with sunshine from dawn to dusk for weeks on end. An occasional shower onto the blanket tenting only at night, dousing the small fire and commanding sleep.

Cloud, Time, and Roger took turns staying awake each night. Time always slept first, with Roger taking the first shift and Cloud taking the second, effectively making Cloud the captain of the night watch. Since she and Roger shared a horse, they took turns dozing while riding. Cloud knew that once Time woke, he would not go back to sleep.

She stood watch the longest, always on her feet. When fatigue made standing unbearable, she would wake Time, who, though a sound sleeper, would be instantly alert. Only then would Cloud sleep until dawn.

Time alternated standing, stretching, and sitting. It's easy to stand when you ride all day, he mused, especially when your arse is chapped and sore. He would wake

Roger an hour or so before dawn. The boy wanted to be useful, and he took to routine and drudgery with a concentration beyond mere duty. He was proving his worthiness with every job assigned, and his tasks included preparing the morning routine with a fire, and then brushing and watering and feeding the horses.

"Soldiers do this, right, Sergeant Time?"

"Yes, Roger, they do." Time never tired of being called sergeant, though his desertion weighed heavier with each new morning.

"Would I be a good soldier?"

Time hesitated. The image of Adam and Goff and the others looking at him the moment of their deaths overwhelmed his consciousness, and Roger could trigger Time's blankness, his catatonic state, just by looking at him with a question.

"Would I?" Innocent, curious, imploring.

"Why, yes, Roger. You have already proven you're brave. And now you have shown you can do what is needed, no matter how repetitious, or, or..."

"Or woman's work."

"Shut up now, your mother may hear you." Time tousled the boy's head playfully.

Sun-up, morning routine, and on the move. As the sun set, depending on the animals and the water supply, the evening bivouac would commence with its usual silence. The girls were cowed by their mother's stern visage. Time, Cloud and Roger hurried their blanket-tent pitching, fire building, and horse tending, the same cycle each day.

Cloud rationed the evening meal and general supplies. Time would glare at her after the dinner food was disbursed in mock anger.

"You're starving me."

Cloud was equal to the humor. "If you ate any more we'd have to kill one of the horses."

The girls at first were horrified, but in the ensuing days the dinner ritual repeated itself, and they played along.

"He might eat one us," said Margaret.

"You'd better stay together, always," said Roger, out of the side of his mouth.

@@@

The ritual of the routine benefits any size family or army, as expectations are direct and consequences, both good and bad, are well known. Routine also harbors grave risk, as complacency in acting by rote will de-sensitize anyone, especially in the absence of concerted and focused leadership.

Time never relaxed. Watching over his band of refugees over the weeks of movement, some days with steady gains, others slow and unproductive, he could feel a paternal pride in their collective and individual purposeful acts, and knew instinctively they all, including Cloud and Mrs. Carmody, maybe especially the two women, craved his approval.

And he suspected they feared that he might not protect them when the time came.

Time would not let sentimentality overcome his sense of impending danger. He was always tired, always exhausted, but he knew he must stay as vigilant as a hawk. He fought the panic that would wave over him whenever a twig snapped or bush rustled. He thought often of his own fear and lack of action the night of Jesse's birth, and saw himself unredeemed the night of Genny's freak death and his murder of the unknown traveler.

"You think I caused her death, don't you?" Time asked her.

Cloud noticed he could not meet her eye, but looked over her head when he finished. It was rare when anyone spoke more than a word or two on the journey, and the open question, one bursting with unsaid accusation and recrimination, triggered something in Cloud she never thought she possessed.

"No," she spat. "You caused *his*. A stranger. You assumed he meant harm, and you didn't know him. I'm no military man," she said each syllable of the words in mock respect, "but we could have asked him, or flanked him, let him explain himself. But, no. You assumed the worst of a stranger, a traveler, like *us*."

"Wait. I am a wanted man. They hang deserters, Missy.'

"Don't *Missy* me. I know you have to protect yourself."

"I'm protecting you!"

"Ha! That isn't working out too well, is it?"

Time could hear the roar in his head, and his eyes glazed and reddened in rage.

Cloud would not relent. "Now you get us north. We'll do better, on our own, there. God willing."

@@@

Thirty days had passed. Time had no map, and he stayed clear of any road and even farther from cultivated property. Much of the journey was on a slope of a ridgeline, and the awkwardness of the horses' movement was exacerbated by Time's tacking of the beasts up and over slopes and fingers and back again and again in order to keep the sun in a steady westward arc.

Normally sensitive to sights and sounds, Time relied heavily on Cloud at the front, while he trailed, passing instructions through a click of the teeth or a soft whistle. The irony amused him, and the girls always smiled on cue.

Complacency, coupled with the horses' natural tendency to step it out on flat terrain, caused the encounter with two Confederate soldiers to escalate into shock and outrage by both parties.

Cloud's mount, at Time's instruction, was to tack right over a grassy ridgeline, the reverse side obscured by what appeared to be dense dark brush. An even stretch of greenery at the apex was inviting for all the horses and the donkey. The riders gave the animals their own lead, right into a pair of Rebel soldiers dozing in the small verdant meadow.

No one moved. Cloud yanked on the reins, and Mrs. Carmody's mount nuzzled the rump of the front horse.

"Now, then. Where you all headed." Not a question, but an accusation from the older soldier.

He rose slowly, not seeing a threat, his hard-lined eyes darting from Time to Cloud and back.

"My brother's place. In Martinsburg. Near there, the old Indian grounds, by the daisy field. You know it?" Mrs. Carmody said sweetly, her shirt open, giving the soldiers the tease of an eyeful of her breasts and swaddled baby.

Time started to dismount before the two soldiers could respond. He wanted to be on the ground if he had to start shooting, knowing the horses would get skittish quickly. The girls bounced down, also.

Roger and Cloud remained motionless.

The younger soldier asked, "I know the place. What's your..."

"I am Katherine Carmody. These are my children." Nodding to Cloud, she stated, "This is my girl."

"And I am her husband, in practice."

The older soldier smiled, with the confidence of seeing weakness, and little thought of a threat.

"I know the place, too. Met your brother once, before the winter. He was worried about all his pigs dying."

Mrs. Carmody snorted and squinted. "He never raised one pig, let alone more than one."

The leader straightened. "I'm Sergeant Mathews, Ma'am. I knows your brother, Mr. Anniston, well. No pigs, dear." He kept glancing at her breasts. "His right eye is all glazed over, now. Lots of sheep and a few cows, he had, last I spoke to 'im." He smiled.

As did Mrs. Carmody. "All right then, sergeant. We just rested so we'll keep moving now."

"Now just a minute. You're not being friendly. We're practically neighbors, unless..."

"Unless what?"

"You're moving a slave north."

"She's mine, mister, and a slave she'll remain," Time's voice was filled with menace, his hand firmly on his rifle grip. The Confederates lost the initiative, gawking at the exchange between Mrs. Carmody's charms and the sergeant's awkwardness.

Time could take both of them if there was any movement.

They all knew it. But only Time knew he could not take the chance.

"We're just bein' hospitality-like."

"You'll not take my property from me." Time's eyes rolled and he started to shake, unnerving the soldiers and the children. He bared his teeth and snarled unintelligibly.

"Whoa, wait, now. We didn't mean nothing..."

"I'll kill her before I let you take her!"

Time swept his rifle to within a foot of Cloud's hip, then slowly arced it up to her head as Roger cringed around the horse's neck.

"Whoa, what, uh, wait there mister!"

Margaret and Anne grabbed at Time's legs. "Look, I'm gonna pass water, then we're leaving, and you're not gonna follow."

"Yeah, sure, sure, no problem!"

Mrs. Carmody looked sidelong at Time, but kept her shirt unbuttoned. Sergeant Mathews and the young soldier, who never stood, were too distracted to think clearly.

"Don't you go moving around. I'm not going far." Time moved the barrel from Cloud to the soldiers and back.

Minutes later the travelers were back on the trail, eyes wide, breathing heavily but silent. Cloud waited a respectable distance, their now collective vigilance on high alert, before she spoke to Time.

"You would have shot me," more to herself than Time.

A peep and a whistle, then, "No!"

"Of course not, Cloud. But they had to think it. And they had to believe I was crazy enough to do it."

"Your eyes scared 'em," Roger mumbled, "Scared me, too."

"Remember. We don't just hate each other. We hate you." He held her glare, winked, and Cloud could not help but smile at him. "We need to protect our supplies and our mounts. To threaten them directly would have been our end." Time was exhausted, weary of the vigilance, the lack of sleep, hoarding water and supplies, and of the fear of being arrested and made chattel of another man's army.

Mrs. Carmody was amused by it all. "He knew my brother, too. He tested me, when he wasn't staring at me."

"How far are we?" Cloud wanted to change the subject.

Time looked up. "We're at least two days away from Martinsburg, but without a map I can't be sure. Couldn't ask those two, but we do need to pick up the pace. The sun is out longer and the ride is pleasant enough," he lied. "We've still got plenty of supplies, so at least we won't show up empty-handed." Time paused. "Your brother will be all right with Cloud, won't he?"

Mrs. Carmody's good mood was quickly broken.

"He'll be fine. It's his shrew wife I don't like. Or his friends. With luck they're off fighting."

An hour later they rested, stretching by a cool, clear stream, the children bathing silently. The baby slept, as did Mrs. Carmody. Time kept watch. Cloud watched Time.

@@@

Three days later they came upon the Martinsburg home of the brother of Mrs. Carmody, Orville Anniston. The supplies brought by the travelers were an unexpected bounty, as Anniston's wife, Esther, was frail and worn and overjoyed to see Anna and all her children, horses and heavy packs.

"We thought you was dead," she gasped, laughing though tears. "Your brother's gone to war, and he took my boy with him." Another sob. "I've barely got the planting done. I need," her shoulders wracked, "I need your help, Katherine, please."

All this before they were dismounted.

"Who else is here?" asked Time.

Less than a generation ago the homestead and fencing were impressive by middle class standards. The house was a mix of log and flat timber, with a wide porch, one and half stories and clear glass windows. A central stone fireplace to keep the place warm in the winter, surrounded by mature trees that would cool it in the summer. A garden large enough to sustain a hungry family, and a horse corral. Two goats munched grass in the only open and unproductive area, from the house to the dirt road. Another tight pen with two dozen sheep. It was still respectable, but a winter without hard work tended to make it appear having gone to seed.

"Just me and my two little girls." Esther Anniston pointed at the porch, where two very chubby girls stood with arms folded and lips pursed.

Time slumped. He would be expected to help this poor woman out.

Mrs. Carmody broke the silence. "Esther, you look a fright. Are you eating?"

She fluttered her hands as if shooing flies. "I have plenty, Katherine, but it's the field work draining me."

Roger whispered to Time, pointing his chin at the girls on the porch. "They's eating all her food and not working, either, I bet."

She heard the boy. "Now, now, they're delicate!" which came out like a rasp.

"You'll eat now, Esther, right this minute, and your daughters will have plenty of field work to do," said Mrs. Carmody, who then handed the baby to Cloud. "There's plenty for all of us to do now!" She strode up the three steps of the porch and directly into the house, followed by Esther and the five children.

Time and Cloud stood by the horses. Time, amused, nudged her. "Families are complicated."

Cloud returned the gesture. "It won't last. Esther will find her mean streak, and I know she has one just by looking at her, and she'll probably fight for her girls' comfort or..."

"Take it out on you." Time finished the thought.

@@@

That evening, after slaughtering an underfed lamb, Time leaned over a fence that corralled three well-fed but poorly exercised horses. He compared them mentally to his own overworked beasts, and gazed over the bounty of livestock and marveled at Esther's good fortune. Most of this farm should have been swallowed up to feed the Rebel army moving through. It appeared that Mr. Orville Anniston was a man to be respected.

"It's a miracle they have this livestock," said Cloud, joining him at the fence.

"Yes, it is. Plenty of green to eat on this little piece of heaven, too."

"You think Esther's husband is an important man?"

"Either that or a dangerous one, with dangerous friends." It would explain the deference of the soldier in the earlier encounter, Time thought.

"Why would this woman allow her daughters to be slothful?" Cloud was disgusted by the rudeness and poor manners at the table, and the lack of respect toward their mother.

"Cloud, you can't explain parents. You were raised by strangers who made you work..."

"But they cared for me!"

"Yes, yes they did. As did mine. But somewhere the strength of the parent gave way to an idleness, a, what's the word?"

"Indulgence."

"Indulgence, yes."

"Those girls are good for nothing and lazy and..."

"Yes, yes, that, too. Don't know why. But Mrs. Carmody has a certain gleam in her eye."

Cloud was not convinced. "I do not trust the situation, Sergeant Time."

Time looked at her directly, and tucked his fingers gently under her chin, raising her face to meet him.

"I know. I think you're right. One night at least, though. One."

Roger bounded up to the fence, wedged himself between Time and Cloud, and hopped onto the top rail, sitting and facing them. He beamed nervously.

"It's safer out here. Mother is barking orders and everybody except Esther is jumping. I ran outta there." The sheep baa'd and the horses neighed in agreement.

Cloud laughed, and Time said, "Thanks for the warning. Let's stay right here."

"Miss Cloud, Momma said she'll keep the baby with her for the night, which I don't understand 'cause she always does anyway. Something else for you about tending to Whistle and Peep... oh, Margaret and Anne. It was kinda strange."

Cloud looked at Time. "The slave girl better get to work." She managed a smile. "At least I'm not cooking and cleaning." Both Cloud and Time knew that Esther would question why the black girl wasn't doing chores. Then she would gossip with neighbors. Cloud hurried off to the house.

There was no moon, but the sky was clear and millions of stars bathed the corrals and the lean sheep full of wool. It had been a long stretch since Time craved tobacco, back in the camp after the battle. He would have killed for a smoke.

In the morning, a transformation. Esther's girls were busy under the watchful eye of Mrs. Carmody, and Margaret and Anne and Roger did routine work they were accustomed to at their mother's direction. Cloud cradled the baby in her shoulder sling, and finished preparing two horses.

Roger noticed and challenged Time. "Are you leaving soon?'

"Yes. Soon. Probably today."

"Why?" Roger almost reached out to Time, but resisted the impulse, which Time noticed.

"Cloud and I have to leave soon, Roger. We can't stay. We're close to Pennsylvania, and I'd feel better if we were farther north. There're Confederate soldiers within a few miles from here, probably a lot closer."

Time gripped the boy's shoulder. "She's at risk, too. I can't abide that."

"What about us? So are we!" Roger struggled to control his anxiety.

"Much less so, Roger. You're here. You're their soldier. You're their man."

"But... but..."

"Did you watch me slaughter that lamb yesterday?"

"Show me again, please. If I'da thought it was the last..."

"Even better, son. I'll let you do it. You're ready."

With the domestic sounds echoing small from the house, Roger shorn the wool of a plump lamb, then killed it, then cleaned it, all under the watchful eye and instruction of Time. It took the entire morning, but Time enjoyed Roger's honesty and eagerness.

"Well done, Roger. Could not have done it better myself."

At noon Cloud and Time were packed and ready to go. Mrs. Carmody was burping an alert Jesse at her shoulder.

"I want to take Jesse with me." Cloud insisted.

Mrs. Carmody had not even considered it. The two women stood, face to face, a single stride apart. Cloud set her feet at shoulder width, her hands clasped under her chin, as if pleading.

But it was a command, filled with righteousness.

Mrs. Carmody barely smiled with her mouth, her eyes saddened. She had grown most attached to the child. Jesse was so good, so easy to please, and the matron did not want to let go.

"She's strong now, Mrs. Carmody. She's my sister's child."

"Oh, Cloud. Oh, dear Jesse." The matron looked out to the trees and hills in the distance, vaguely aware Esther was watching with equal measures of curiosity and suspicion. Mrs. Carmody thought of all this girl went through. Tending to two headstrong boys killed in battle. Clinging to a child-like friend, a sister, and protecting her from all of life's unfairness, except not from a boy who would get her pregnant. The company of a rough savior whose personal fears and demons would accidently lead to her sister's death. And Jesse's birth being the greatest achievement of Genevieve's simple and hard life. If Cloud left now, without the baby, she would have less than nothing of her life as she knew it.

Nothing of her adopted family, who must love her with a painful intensity even in death.

Mrs. Carmody kissed the baby's forehead, and gently nudged Jesse's head from her shoulder, and that was all the encouragement Cloud needed. She grabbed for the child, held her close, breathed deeply of the sweetness of the baby's crown, mouthed a *thank you* to Mrs. Carmody, and turned quickly to her horse as her eyes brimmed.

Time shook his head. "Miss Cloud..."

"Not a word Sergeant Time. I'll never leave this baby. Ever. I'll stay here and fight and die first."

Time sighed heavily, shoulders slumped.

"Get on your horse, first. I'll hand the child to you."

@@@

A day passed, and they were in Pennsylvania. Travelers and homesteaders greeted them, and when Cloud asked for milk or soft cheese or other foodstuffs, people were friendly and generous. One traveler told Time that he and Cloud were headed east, directly on the road to Philadelphia, but that the railroad was generally due north, on the road to Harrisburg.

"You go east, there's risk. Why aren't you traveling at night?"

"We aim for Philadelphia. I have family there. And this girl is no slave."

"And she's no mother, either. Your baby?"

"Yes." Lying came easily. Time thought it best to complete others' stories and expectations rather than give too much food for thought. People accepted what they assumed to be true.

"Well, stay on the main road, then. Plenty of working farms that can provide for you, if the need arises." They had these small conversations all day.

"Hello, neighbor. How far to Philadelphia?"

"You're about 150 miles, an easy seven day ride."

"Good, good, say, what's the date?"

"The fifteenth of June. A pretty month, don't you think?"

"My favorite."

"Shouldn't you be riding at night?"

"In a hurry, friend, thanks for the guidance."

And on it went. They slept outdoors. Cloud fussed mightily preparing nourishment for the baby, with cow or goat's milk. Jesse didn't cry from hunger or cramping, though. Time suspected the baby knew it was deeply loved, and safe.

@@@

11
Philadelphia

When they arrived in Philadelphia, Time sold the horses and his only rifle, keeping the pistol. They stayed in low rent rooms in different places the first three nights, looking for bargains and without establishing connections. They rose early and walked the streets to get accustomed to the city, and to find suitable food for the baby. Time forgot how much he did not miss city life, and was intimidated in that he did not know this one at all.

Cloud was in awe. But her first and only concern was Jesse's welfare.

The city street will take its sacrifices at night, from those inattentive or foolish or careless, yet during the light it takes randomly from the innocent in order to claim its dominion from all who try to conquer its shrine to false progress. Cities have their own cloying evil, a badness that seeks the weak, and preys on the weakest.

On the fourth day the morning mist lifted quickly, though the wet of the street in mud and stone clung to the boots and feet of those who were either finishing their night or starting their day. It was warm for late June in Philadelphia, the streets and alleys sloping to the river in a steady bend that was un-level and required caution.

Time assumed that food merchants would be near the piers at the waterfront. Easy marks for theft or generosity would be there, too, and Time had little hesitation to do what was necessary to secure food and shelter for Cloud and Jesse. They were his first priority. Nothing was beneath him now. Fatigue, hunger, and a hopeless spirit consumed his judgment and spat out what little remained of his humanity.

Time had no plan, and that was never good.

Street vendors began setting up shop. Fruit, nuts, almost no vegetables, dried meat of indeterminate kind, and many flowers. A large cart of axe-cut green wood, pulled by two large men, filthy and slick with sweat even at this cool early hour, stopped in a self-assigned spot near an old woman with blankets piled in her lap. Her yellow eyes were wide with fatigue and her toothless grin reflected her own fear.

One side of the alley had a gutter, wide as a man's shoulders, that began somewhere in the city, broadened through the market, then narrowed again as it spilled toward the Delaware River a hundred yards away, dropping more steeply as it emptied. The gutter ran purposefully downhill through the market. There was no room for livestock or horses. Vendors kept to the opposite side. The night people mingled with the morning people and politeness was silent though crowded.

@@@

A boarding house several long hidden blocks uphill from the market trapped rainwater on its roof, and its cistern was full. The proprietor needed to reduce the weight daily when it rained, and when guests were plenty they used his collected water with abandon. Today he had a half empty house of late sleepers. With an indifferent heave, he opened his spillover valve for a half drain, and water cascaded down the sluice toward the street gutter hard enough to take a careless man off his feet. As he opened the valve, his hand slipped and slid on a dry board, embedding a large splinter in his palm. This is bad, he thought, I need to work this out now.

He ignored the draining cistern.

@@@

At the market, three Marines were finishing their night. Still in dress uniform though worse for wear, they fought exhaustion with the bawdy humor of a lingering intoxication and spotty memory. One older Marine, a sergeant, looked fresh and still nearly perfectly creased, but his blood-shot eyes and hard-lined bloodless face gave him away.

"The sun's up laddies; time to call it a night."

The other two Marines were barely out of their teens, their uniforms ill-fitted, and they nodded assent, though they looked with an exhausted fascination at the leather goods, home-made knives, and assorted foods from the vendors. They were in no hurry for their night to end, and stood by the old woman with the blankets.

"Kane, don't get any ideas. You broke one heart last night, I'll not stand for another," chided the salty sergeant. All three Marines laughed soundlessly, remembering antics from a few hours earlier.

"I'll forever protect m' lady's honor," said Kane, who bowed stiffly and stood unsteadily.

The sergeant was getting less amused as the morning warmth descended. "Slenko, grab him. Let's get moving. For a couple new recruits, you two are not worth the trouble."

Slenko shrugged and smiled. "Right you are, sergeant, by all accounts." He laughed and threw an arm over Kane's shoulders.

Cloud held the baby tightly in a sling, and Jesse slept. Time stood in the shadows of the alley, looking for the right contact for quick and profitable work and a secure place to keep themselves, in order to make their money last. The three Marines gave him pause. He could tell they were coming off a binge but knew his presence might elicit a remark, then a retort, then a challenge. He would wait for them to continue their walk downhill to the river.

Two mulatto women walked arm in arm with wide empty baskets and were fixated on the plants and flora. They began pointing and inquiring even before the displays were ready. The flower merchants, children not yet in their teens, hollow eyed yet eager, began the barter, and the alley came alive with chatter as if a bell had rung.

A hooded figure, tall and dark, stepped into the alley from the shadows not far from Time. His gnarled hands, broken by a lifetime of work, held an instrument above his head, displayed for everyone who could hear him.

He startled the Marines and Time. They saw him holding aloft a mandolin, and listened to the hooded man speak in a sonorous sing-song cadence.

"Look at this body, full, tanned, sleek in presentation, people! Delicate though durable, almost wet in appearance, but shining from the promise of what strong and practiced hands can elicit from her! Beautiful to look upon, but only a few can draw the purpose of her existence, the intricacies of sound and vibration that tear the heart and lift the spirit of those who are honored to listen to her; but," and he paused for breath, bringing his tone to a lower more intimate level, yet still well above the murmur around him, "the soul of he who plays her, pinches the strings, plucks the chords, holds her neck gently and her body with possession, and looks upon her as she sings under his hands, will be blessed with the memory created and forever playing for him, for all time."

The Marines and Time stared, mute. Most of the crowd ignored the hooded man, and the vendors shook their heads in mild disgust. He had tried to draw the attention of those with money, and the whispers of ill-gotten gains, of the mandolin having been stolen, began.

Cloud was unfazed, believing that the hooded man held something of real beauty and value, far beyond the capacity and finances of the present low clientele of this farmer's market in an uneven alley.

The suddenness of the chatter and the man's speech woke Jesse, and Cloud began to soothe her. The baby was hungry, insistent, and curious. Cloud gingerly put the child on her shoulder.

She almost called Time by his rank, and smiled inwardly.

"Master Time."

Cloud did not fully appreciate his need for anonymity in a city he never set foot in. She resolved to find humor in small things today, and then good fortune would shine on them, like the early morning sun now on her cheeks, even if the blessing was only a smile from a stranger.

"Master Time."

Time stepped from the shadows, still fogged by the mandolin barker, and he looked down at Cloud. No one heard her but him, the noise of the market drowning her joke.

"Very funny, young lady." He suppressed too wide a grin.

"I don't see any ready food here," she said with renewed gravity, "Should we continue down the hill, or go back up?" Cloud was looking at the baby she held, and then glanced down toward the river. Time looked back up the alley, sighed, and started the walk uphill. He thought he saw the street move at the crest, and shook his head, believing exhaustion was playing tricks with his eyes, the early sun reflecting off, and cutting through, the shadows.

An auburn haired girl in her early teens was holding two younger children by the hand, all poorly dressed. Their freckled faces and light wispy hair told the story of a big sister leading younger siblings for an early walk. Perhaps they would find scraps or work or a handsome soldier to flirt with, the girl thought. The little boy fidgeted mightily and tried to throw her hand away, and they both struggled and fought each other for supremacy, hissing and staring with feigned malevolence, as young siblings do. The boy didn't need his sister to hold his hand, he kept saying. He was bigger than the flower merchants and they were working, he spat. Holding his sister's hand completed his public humiliation.

The little girl, barely three years old, sucked her thumb, stared at the normalcy of her older siblings toward each other, and held her sister's hand with gentle confidence. The disagreement bored her, and she looked uphill.

The Marine sergeant started walking in a long stride downhill, but was nagged by an unfamiliar sound, lower than the steady chattering of the crowd. He turned to face first the mandolin man, spied Time, and looked uphill. The sound grew louder.

Time stared at the sergeant, then followed his gaze up the alley.

Water burst atop the gutter, bulging over the sides, rushing faster and in higher volume than if from a thunderstorm. It poured in a nearly two foot funnel down the gutter, and the first person to react before it rushed past the crowd was the little girl, who pointed at it just as it hit her in the face and swept her away.

Cloud watched it happen.

"Dear Lord."

She thrust Jesse into Time's chest, who now looked down and watched the torrent not three strides away. Cloud could see the child's arm flail, and her periphery took in the shoppers struggling to maintain their collective feet.

Cloud dove into the gutter and it, too, took her away.

Time tried to follow and he lost his footing, and fell on his back, not knowing that Cloud went after a child. He clung to Jesse, and sat in a shallow pool created by the still rushing water.

Cloud forced her arms in front of her, and stiffened her back and legs, trying to reach the girl now only a few feet away. The child's hair, wet and black and stringy, was all Cloud could see of her.

The river was in sight, the drop off to it sharp and unseen. If the girl goes over that edge, Cloud thought, she'll never be found. Cloud willed herself forward, faster, throwing her wrists outward in desperation.

At the crest the flow of water slowed enough for the child's arms and legs to come into view. The girl's wide eyes looked right into Cloud's, and the girl shrieked and tumbled over the edge just as Cloud gripped a full handle of hair.

Cloud dug her knees and toes into the gutter, but its slipperiness prevented effective purchase. She saw in an instant a horrific drop, forty or fifty feet, onto water beaten piles of wood, pier legs, trash and rocks. The gutter didn't follow the road to the river. It emptied into a cavernous dump.

Cloud was going over.

I will not die, she thought. Grab something...

She fell over the edge, and an iron bar or large nail was right in front of her, missing the girl's head by an angel's breath. Cloud thrust out her hand, but the bar slid past, and now her hips and legs were pushing her into a somersault.

Cloud screamed. The girl shrieked louder, her hands beating at Cloud's grip on her hair. In desperation, Cloud hooked her free arm where she thought the bar or nail would be, and it sunk into her upper arm.

They stopped. Water flew over them. The slapping sound on the rocks below was louder than the shouts just a few feet above them, where the street turned and the gutter ended.

Cloud's arm was impaled on a large nail on a bar of iron. A ferocious pain shot through her, and she almost released her grip on the child, who continued to shriek in pain from the grip on her hair. Cloud could feel the child's scalp give a little every second the waterfall continued to hammer them. She could not pull the girl up.

"Grab a leg." A whisper.

The child kept screaming and flailing.

"Stop that right now young lady!" Cloud saw reason would fail, so she opted for brazen authority.

"Grab my leg or I'll pull all your hair out!"

Cloud swung her leg to the girl, and after gently kicking her, the child hugged Cloud at the knee.

"Good girl! Good girl!"

The water stopped.

"Hey Missy, Missy! What happened?"

Cloud glanced up, wincing. Three heads were looking over the edge where the sluice ended and the alley turned away. Three lean faces, unshaven, in uniforms.

The older one said to her, "What's holding you up?"

Cloud groaned. The pain was in her shoulders, neck, and head, and her eyes hurt. She couldn't look up anymore.

"I'm on a nail, I think, under my arm. On it good and deep." Cloud tried to look up again, but failed and hung her head and gazed at the girl gripping her leg with both of her arms and legs, frozen and wild-eyed.

"The girl, she's..." Cloud wanted to sleep.

"Wait, wait, don't do that, talk to me."

Time was at the edge, the old fear creeping onto him. He had passed Jesse to a curious woman.

"Cloud, Cloud, stay there."

She smiled and thought, I'm not going anywhere, not without this little girl who hates me. She could hear Time and the older Marine shouting at each other. The other two, young uniformed men, reached for her but missed by several arms' lengths.

The sergeant shouted to her, "Can you grab a rope?"

Cloud's head hung, the pain too acute to force a look upward. She stared at the girl, and at the wood and piles and rocks below.

"No."

At the edge, Kane told Slenko to hold his legs. The two Marines scrambled to position themselves, while the sergeant and Time held Slenko. The surface was still slick with water and grease and grime, and the men were unsure of how to get the job done but certain they had to do something right now.

The crowd pressed to the edge, curiosity compelling them forward to see what was out of view. There was nothing to see until one could look over the edge, but that didn't stop the now two dozen on-lookers from trying to watch what was happening.

"Back off! There's nowhere to go here!" The sergeant was fuming, gasping and spitting at the surge.

Kane reached his hands out, trusting the grip at his own legs, but still could not reach Cloud's head. She tried to look up at him, sensing the nearness.

"Hurry." The strain on her arm and shoulder was more pronounced, and the weight of the child clutching her leg was growing heavier by the second.

The hooded man, the mandolin man, was at the sergeant's side.

"Use this," he whispered, handing him a sturdy rope. The sergeant shouted at the discovery.

"Pull him up, boys!" The sergeant looped one end of the gifted rope around Kane's waist, securing it with a square knot and two half-hitches.

"This won't go anywhere. Can you handle the anchor, sir?"

Time nodded, and the sergeant guessed the length needed, and wrapped the balance of the rope around the middle of Time's chest, Slenko now feeding tense line to lower Kane to the hanging Cloud. Another surge from the crowd.

"Back off, people, back off! There's no room here, nothing to see!"

Slenko sat, crouched in front of Time, whose legs were spread wide, heels dug into the slick surface, begging for purchase anywhere. Slenko nodded to Kane, who slowly rolled off the edge. Time and Slenko jolted from the weight, but the knot held firm. Kane laughed.

"Sometimes being smaller is pretty good, huh?"

"Hurry."

Slenko fed rope a few inches at a time, grip firm and steady.

"This will be heavier when he grabs her," he barked over his shoulder.

Time was ready. "We'll prevail, son."

Kane was now eye to eye with Cloud, whose gaze was glassy and unfocused.

"Can you reach out to me?"

"My arm. I think it landed on a nail." She smiled.

The girl sneezed, then sniffled, her grip now tighter.

The hooded man's hand was on Time's shoulder, whose grip on the rope was firm and confident. He had no problem as the anchor. Slenko's purchase was also solid, though as he perspired his hands became slick. Time bent the rope to his hip, looping his wrist in the momentary slack.

Slenko barked, "Let's do this now, Kane."

And the sergeant was airborne.

The crowd sensed something grand was to happen, and the insensibility of curiosity for its own sake consumed the mob of on-lookers and critics. For all his effort the sergeant couldn't control the wave of people, and in his own craning to see Kane finally reaching the woman and child he lost his awareness and his footing.

And he was airborne.

The mob gasped.

The hooded man rose his arms and stepped back, forcing the surge away from the edge.

Cloud cried out.

The sergeant turned in the air and faced the sky and his Marines and looked into the eyes of Heaven.

"*Hold your position*!" And with that he landed flatly and messily and crumbled on the debris fifty feet below, instantly gone.

Kane's eyes never left Cloud's.

"Missy, look at me."

"Yes."

"We can only go up, now."

Slenko's torrent of curses was exceeded only by his need to know. He called to his sergeant.

"Sergeant Hawkins? Sergeant Hawkins? Are you all right? Kane, is he all right? I can't see him!"

Kane never looked down. He had heard the finality of the sickening thud of impact.

"He's gone, Slenko. You heard him. Hold steady."

The hooded figure rose to his full height, spun to face the mob of insipid and curious, and pulled the hood back from his head. Anger radiated from his eyes and his nostrils flared. Baring his teeth, he spat in the air above the crowd's heads. The mob recoiled from his visage and raw physical power, and everyone took several steps back in guilt and fear.

"Fools! You've killed a man! You had to see, but offered nothing! You had to criticize, but are not committed!"

He pointed directly at too large and boisterous men, instigators.

"You've killed a man trying to save a woman and child. Would you kill them, too?"

The men tried to curl into themselves, shamed.

The dark circles under the eyes of the cloaked man now bore into three women who still appeared to be trying to loom over the edge. He pointed now to them.

"What can you do now? Do you want to see more death here on your street? Do you want to join him?" His tone was malevolent. "That is the only view I can offer *you*."

He pointed over the straining heads of Time and Slenko, and over the edge.

"There, you miserable hags, do you want to look... closely?" The threat was not hidden. The man was inviting them to go over the edge and join the now broken and dead form of the Marine sergeant.

He drew in his breath, and shouted over the heads of the now docile crowd.

"Save yourselves, first! Your darkest heart to witness has caused this good man's death. Save yourselves, for you cannot save him!"

The crowd, eyes cast down, parted as two policemen came running up.

"What goes on here?" An elderly overweight cop in a uniform too tight and long faded wheezed at the cloaked man, who only shook his head, pulled his hood over his crown, and walked up the street.

Time shouted, "There's a woman and a small girl caught on a piece of timber ten feet down. We're holding a Marine by rope to rescue. One Marine fell below... I think he's dead."

"Aye, he's gone," said Slenko, evenly, with a mix of pride and disgust, as only a man who has endured the witness and anguish of a useless death can express.

Kane had finished inspecting Cloud's arm wound. His probes had been gentle but quick, displaying an all-business and no waste approach to a task he was ill prepared for, coupled with the awkward suspension of a rope held by unseen hands.

"Okay, Missy."

"Cloud."

"No, no clouds, look at me."

"No, my name is Cloud."

"Oh, yes, very good Missy. I am Private Kane, United States Marine Corps." He thought her delirious. "I think it's a nail, and your arm is flat on it. Not much blood, as I can see. I'll lift you off, and I'll hold you. Hook your other arm around my neck."

"No! I have the girl!"

"Right, Missy, yes. I have you now." Kane then shouted to be heard above: "I'll bear her weight now. Hold your..." and he trailed off, aware in that instant the last words of his sergeant.

"...Position!" Called Slenko, who redoubled his grip, and Time secured his hips and heels in the loose stones; the policemen bear-hugged Time and leaned back, eyes wide, assisting without seeing or understanding the danger. The rope bit hard into Time's hands.

"Now, Missy, now!"

Kane put both his arms around Cloud, and called out, "Heave up a couple feet," and as the rope tightened he felt the pull off the beam, and lifted Cloud off the nail.

She came off clean. They hung for a moment in the air.

"Bring us up, we're free!"

Kane bear-hugged Cloud, Cloud fisted the hair of the girl, and the girl seized Cloud's leg.

The rope moved slowly up, Slenko and Time pulling mightily inch by inch. The fat cop, grabbing under Time's shoulder and straining, said, "Perhaps you stand and walk backwards."

"Perhaps you shut up and hold."

Slenko saw Kane within inches of his grasp.

"I need two men on me now. Just two."

The men shamed by the cloaked man rushed forward, their knees at the edge. They did not look down. They grabbed the rope, steady and dry, and now five men pulled and walked away from the edge.

Slenko tried to grip the rope around Kane's torso.

"No, try to grab her, the child."

Yet the men had to keep pulling, and Kane turned facing away from the edge, scraping his uniform coat, ripping it on the rock and stones which cut hard into his back.

Slenko grabbed Kane under his shoulders, firmly. Kane turned, now on his knees next to Slenko, and gingerly placed Cloud and the child into Time's arms.

Cloud shouted, "Jesse!"

The auburn haired girl rushed forward and hugged the ragged, wet, and frightened little one, who cried out, "Oh Sissy, oh Sissy I almost fell," and she burst into fresh tears. Cloud released her entwined hand from the girl's matted hair.

As Kane and Slenko knelt by Time's side, Cloud sobbed and begged for Jesse, tears welling, imploring Time, the pain beginning to overwhelm her. Time crushed her to his chest.

A woman ran up. "Here's the baby." She held Jesse out to Time. "She's fine. Slept the whole time. I have to go now. God bless you." She looked at Time alone.

@@@

Kane sat at the edge, and Slenko knelt on his haunches beside him. They looked down into the pit, and as the sun had risen higher shards of light illuminated the buttons on the dress coat of the broken and lifeless form of Sergeant Hawkins.

Slenko would not take his gaze from his sergeant below. He had spent the night drinking with him, the man who told Slenko he was born to be a Marine. Kane, too, who on a city street now fully understood the bond of trust between sergeant and private, how serving honorably sometimes meant acting outrageously, taking risks, and being heedless of personal safety. That Missy Cloud would be a fine Marine, Kane mused silently; it took balls to dive down that sewer gutter after a child, and then fall over the edge, unknowing into the unknown. Iron balls.

Sergeant Hawkins would have approved.

"We have to go get him. Now."

@@@

It took an hour to secure and lift the sergeant from his awkward repose in death. The police were in charge at this point, and the day was working against them. The tidal pressure of the river was making the water rise in the pit, and the flow had started to touch the sergeant's hand. It was decided to clear the street of gawkers first, and then try to loop the end of the rope around either an arm or a leg.

The two Marines protested. Violently. Time came to the policemen's aid, and stopped what would have been a beating.

"He's right, Slenko. There's barely enough rope to get to him, not enough to drop anyone down there and bring 'em both back up. Let's get the slipknot right, first. The day's wasting."

Slenko was resigned to the losing battle. "Kane, you tie the knot, I'll show you." Kane stood taller, and Slenko pointed and critiqued as the rope twisted under the young Marine's hands. Slenko was resigned to remembering his sergeant through the greatest honor: assuming his mantle of leadership by teaching the new man.

@@@

Time, hands raw and cut, carried Cloud, who cradled Jesse. The teen sister carried the little girl and the restless boy skipped ahead.

"I'm hungry." The little one chirped. Time laughed.

A doctor had been summoned earlier and ministered to Cloud with no hesitation in the street, and the prognosis was good, a deep but clear puncture under the bicep, but otherwise not torn.

"First time I have ever seen such a wound and thought it was good fortune, Miss," said the doctor, a gentleman by his clothes, and an angel by his manner. "It will take many weeks, but it should heal without major effect."

With that the doctor departed, walking leisurely away with the hooded figure, the doctor holding the mandolin as if it were a baby.

@@@

Another hour passed. Cloud was now walking and wore a bright green kerchief over her head, and a deep sky blue knit shawl. On another woman the colors would have drained her, but on Cloud the contrast was striking, and her eyes danced whenever she moved her head. The three children orbited around Time, who held Jesse.

Cloud smiled broadly, turning her shoulders and looking at her reflection in the shop window in a sidelong glance that tried to flirt with reflected spirits. The two Marines smiled with her, proud of their gifts to this tiny woman.

"You are pretty as a picture, Missy."

"Oh, stop." Cloud was not used to being the coquette.

"You take my breath away, Miss Cloud," said Kane, exaggerating a bow and a flourished off head sweep of his cover.

And Slenko could not stop talking. Cloud smiled, the children were in rapt attention, Time pretended not to hear, and Kane kept shaking his head.

"There's a song like that, 'Breath Away', if I recall. Oh, my father sang with gusto. My own brothers and sister tried to sing in tune, and I pretended to know the words. A happy man, my father, he was. My mother was Methodist and my father was moldable. A good life." Slenko would not tire.

Kane was growing impatient. "We need to attend to the sergeant, Slenko. The authorities should be finished with their work."

Time, exhausted, was ready to call it a day, and did not want to attract any more attention than the situation required. He marched up, and cradled both Jesse and the little rescued girl, Sarah. "Let's get these children home, Cloud. They seem quite content now."

The children's faces were tear-streaked and chocolate smeared, as candy will overcome fear in most cases. Time began to hand Sarah to Cloud, and the girl was already pushing away from him and nearly leapt into Cloud's arms.

"That's my little princess. Are you ready to go home now?"

Sarah hummed happily, her older sister and brother looking at Cloud in unbridled awe.

"Please come home with us, Cloud! Father will be so happy to meet you!"

The Marines took their leave, wishing Cloud and Time and the children all the good graces God could offer them. Cloud promised to pray for them, and for the soul of Sergeant Hawkins. They stood silently, and Time led Cloud and the children away, the Marines watching them walk slowly down the street.

The afternoon sun was beginning its descent. Time squinted directly into the white beacon, seeking its warmth and promise of life, his eyes wholly opened and aware of his own loneliness. James Time was orphaned in mind and spirit, thoughts and actions drifting to anywhere and nowhere, looking for succor of purpose and crushed by his fatigue and the uncertainty of fate. The orphan keeps moving on, he thought, and in that motion finds peace in the chaos of the unknown and its insecurity, the dream that whatever challenge, fight, or terror that awaits him, it is better than the void of being unloved.

Several long and uneven blocks later, the children ran up the steps of a tenement, one that stood out for a neatness and cleanliness unmatched by its neighboring buildings. The girl and boy were shouting, though little Sarah remained attached to Cloud. By the time Cloud and Time reached the door, a middle aged man, dressed in working clothes, stood astonished and grinned.

"Praise God! I had heard of a ruckus and prayed it weren't mine own, but Lord! It be!

"Come in, come in, and oh, do come in! Sarah, darling, Sarah, you forget your pap so soon?" To Time alone, hand extended, "I'm Thomas Mahoney!"

And Sarah was passed to her father, and her tears flowed knowing that he would melt when he held her.

During the course of the day the children countered the reports Mr. Mahoney had heard, Time tried to fill gaps, and Jesse squealed in hunger until a buxom woman scooped her up and began to feed her a few feet away in another room, Cloud eyeing the open door where Jesse was taken. The nursing woman would not go too far away, as the whole neighborhood buzzed with the heroics of the black girl and her sullen companion. After the story was exhausted, Mahoney told his family's tale, of his wife's infirmity and his own sister's loss, which became the saving grace of Jesse. Mahoney was fascinated with Cloud's speech and language mastery, impressed with vocabulary as any man with little formal education would be. When he asked where Cloud and Time and Jesse were staying, he sensed their hesitation immediately, as any hard-working man is sensitive to the needs of those who have nothing.

"You'll both stay here! The baby can't go anywhere! And your arm must heal!"

Time protested, but Cloud did not. She offered to tutor his children for room and board for herself and the baby, which was enthusiastically seconded by the matron who was nursing Jesse. Her bark from the other room shook the window glass, and Time suspected that she was relieved and grateful. Time had also counted three other urchins running about, and he suspected that the matron had her hands full, and that Cloud would have no problem with them at all.

"Well! It's settled, then!" Every exhortation from Mahoney burst forth as a shout.

"I'll be taking my leave tonight, sir. After dark." Time stated it flatly.

"But your child..."

Another tale from Time, with necessary truths. More wide eyes, and Cloud's high spirit began to fade.

"Now, now, Miss Cloud, you're our family now," said Mahoney, patting and rubbing his hand on Sarah's head, as she slept on his lap. He cooled noticeably toward Time. There were limits to a father's gratitude. The desertion from war. To a man like Mahoney who was serving and had one precious week of leave, it was unforgivable for anyone healthy of Time's age, even if a former Confederate. Mahoney had not been told all of it, as Time suspected that the gregarious father would be much less solicitous to a murderer.

@@@

After a modest lamb but mostly potato supper, the new family dynamic was established with rough and casual precision, riding on the euphoria of Cloud's heroism. She and Time stood out in the street, he with a small pack slung over his shoulder.

"What the hell were you thinking?"

Cloud wheeled on him, incensed, "No one tells me what I can and cannot or should or should not do! I decide! I know right from wrong and watching that girl drown in a sewer was wrong!"

Time was taken aback at the ferocity in the woman's words, her eyes flashing, teeth clenched, and fists shaking.

He softened his remonstrance. "You could have died."

Cloud's shoulders sank, and her once proud countenance crashed into Time's chest. She would have sobbed, but she had nothing left. Cloud inhaled slowly and deeply, and then let it all out in a rush.

"It would have been wrong to watch her die."

Time thought about all the men he had watched die, sometimes at his hand. Other times he was unable to act, wishing he, too, had the presence of mind, the audacity, to act with his conviction so swiftly.

"If you had died, what about Jesse?"

"You would have spent forever watching over her." Cloud pulled her head up to look at this broken man, placing her hands on his chest, just as Genevieve had done months before.

"I know, Cloud. Hear my heart."

Cloud chuckled. "And use your head. If you only listen to your heart you may be jumping into a lot of open sewers."

Time wanted to laugh, but could not. He knew that he would jump into a hundred cesspools before he would care for a baby. A thousand.

She looked up at him. "Thank you, James Time. You are my hero. Always."

"You are very complicated, Cloud Parker. I will forever bear the burden of Genny's death. Your forgiveness is divine."

"No, no, that was fate, James. Fear not for me. I will be quite content here, for a while. Perhaps they'll adopt Jesse."

"Yes, I will pray they shall. Good people. Loud, but good." They both smiled.

The silence was broken only when Time placed both hands on Cloud's shoulders, and leaned forward, pecking her brow with gentleness. As he leaned back, Cloud folded herself under his arms, squeezing tightly with her right, tenderly with her left.

"You'll be fine, Cloud, I know it."

"Thank you, James Time. Go with God."

@@@

12
Going West

Time walked toward the setting sun. He was torn between his sense of responsibility and his long sought freedom, but knew now his greatest obligation had been securing the safety of the little Jesse and Cloud. The job was done. Time felt no relief.

He had failed Jesse Moas' mother, the innocent Genevieve. He had failed the two boys, Goff and Adam. He failed an entire company of boy soldiers, his orphans; he left his last friend, Corporal Garadon, to an unknown fate. He had murdered a man who was only in the wrong place at the wrong time.

He had also brought justice where he saw fit, and he was still unrepentant for hanging Mother Corn, though it was not enough to comfort his anguish and it was too consuming to ignore.

"Where are you headed?" Someone called out.

The voice sat on a wagon of assorted covered supplies large enough for three men to sleep in. The two-horse team was rested and restless and ached to move, being held in check by a mountain of a man, as wide as he appeared tall on the driver bench. He gripped the reins with one hand, fully in control of both horses. A powerful man who knew it.

Time stopped walking. The man's smile was crooked but friendly, and he held Time's eyes, silently commanding a response.

"Down this road. Nowhere in particular."

"Well," and the teamster cracked his neck in a swirl, yapping out a yawn. "I could use company. Have to get this load to market, and I may have to drive all night."

Time barely heard the man. He stared at the unlit cigar in the teamster's free hand, still marveling at how he could hold two straining horses in one hand.

The driver's brow began to perspire. "Look, get on. If'n you bore me too much, I'll just throw you off." The man and horses snorted in unison.

Time could picture in his mind being thrown for an impressive distance from the wagon seat by this mountain.

Time half-smiled. "Sorry, neighbor, I am lost in my own troubles."

The driver chortled. "Fair enough. Get on. By the time I tell you all mine you'll jump off yourself."

Time climbed aboard, extending his hand.

"I'm Time. Jim Time."

"I'm McDavitt. Call me Mac." He threw his cigar into his mouth and gripped Time's hand like a vice. Time flinched, and before McDavitt would move the horses he flipped Time's hand over to inspect it.

"Good Lord, Mr. Time, your hands are a fright! They should be bandaged." He snapped the reins and the horses started to move.

Time stared into his hands. He had not felt them acutely until now. Red, raw, cut and split. They would be too swollen to work in a day, perhaps infected if they were not tended to soon.

"I have just the thing for you. I bought a hand balm from a comely lass today, a tiny thing, truly, with the most, the most, amazing charms," McDavitt extended his hands far from his own chest. "She was selling these tins of this magic formula that fill the cracks made on a working man's hands and makes 'em soft and tender. She was beautiful!" He extended his hands again, as if Time had not already taken interest. "I could have watched, uh, listened to her all day, which explains my late start." He handed a tin from his coat pocket to Time.

"So you bought two tins from her."

"Two?! I bought ten!"

Time threw his head back, and roared. He had not felt that shocking an explosion of real mirth in ages, and it felt good to release all his troubles and doubt in several booming guffaws. He began to lose his breath, and his eyes glistened unbidden. McDavitt was laughing, too.

"Rub that stuff into your hands Mr. Time, and I guarantee you'll feel better. Good Lord I wish you could have been there. She rubbed my hands so well I begged her to marry me. Which would have been a shock to my missus."

Now Time was losing control over himself, and his laughter became silent and insistent, heedless of what McDavitt thought or what the occasional pedestrian might think. He scooped the cream from the tin and gingerly rubbed it with his fingers into one palm. The effect was immediate.

"Oh. Oh my goodness. This is wonderful! It stinks to high heaven, though."

"Get used to it. You'll need it, and sometimes you take the good with the bad. I didn't smell anything until you mentioned it, and well, I was feasting my eyes... Ah, the smile of a happy woman holds the promise of love: this is God's greatest gift to man."

"And this balm is the second greatest gift. I can feel the healing, immediately."

"Ha! That it is! The picture now, of the girl's prodigious chest underneath a buck-toothed grin is enough to make all your pain go away, I gather!"

Time smiled broadly. "Yes, it is all easing away, Mac, though I can't help feeling a little selfish."

McDavitt snorted in exaggerated derision. "No sense being miserable when the world still holds such wonderment. Ah, yes. Such wonder..."

Their giddiness slowed down after a few minutes and they settled into silence. Time's hands now felt immeasurably better, and McDavitt focused on his unlit cigar, keeping the horses moving and avoiding the normal twilight obstacles on the road west and out of Philadelphia.

McDavitt did not like the silence.

"I know you have troubles, Jim, but I'll be damned if I can read 'em. Maybe a woman, maybe a child, maybe you're just tired. But one of us has to talk, friend, 'cause we'll be moving all night."

Time grunted a cough, a half-hearted laugh.

"I'm all ears, Mac."

"Good, then. You seem to have shaken a burden, Jim. A burden you just assume to have kept carrying. In fact..."

"Wait a minute. You gonna talk about me? I don't even need the ride."

McDavitt snapped his wrists, a gentle tap and release to his team.

"Be easy, friend. I'm an observer. My story is boring and doesn't count. So I'll make one up about you!"

Time turned sharply to the teamster, feet firm to the buckboard. "Well, I'll be. I was minding my own business, practically sleeping on my feet. Now I'm wide awake. You have my attention. What is it you see in a broken old soldier?"

McDavitt pulled the cigar from his mouth, and looked at the unlit end as if for the first time.

"Soldier, huh?"

Time suspected the words were in condemnation.

"Yes. On a leave, of sorts."

"Where's your rifle?" McDavitt's tone was flat, hollow.

"Long gone. I..." Time sighed and shook his head, and turned away to face the not quite full moon in the night sky, its reflection beating down on his face, the horses, and the road ahead.

"We have all night, Mr. Time. Best tell me before we get where we're going."

"It'll cost you a cigar." Time thought he should be reasonable, and he smiled in some pain behind his eyes, his hands feeling like duck down.

McDavitt grinned broadly, reached into his coat, and produced by all appearances a very fine cigar.

"That's the spirit, Jim. That's more like it."

Time bit down, chewed off the end, and spat the small nub away. Mac was quick with the match for Time, and then lit his own soggy piece, drawing on it with some effort. They both puffed fully, rapidly, and enjoyed the burn and the aroma.

"That is more like it, Mac. Thanks. I didn't catch your first name."

"I didn't tell it. Just been Mac for me since I was a child, as I recall."

"Why? Your name Mary or something?"

"Ha! Well, Jim Time, that is more like it!" They grinned in unison.

Time puffed, relaxed his shoulders, and he could feel the balm work its magic on his hands. He scooped more and rubbed it liberally, leaving an extra coat from his fingertips to his wrists, palm and knuckles, all. He decided to enjoy the moonlight, the cigar, and the camaraderie of a stranger who wanted nothing from him but his presence.

"What're you hauling, Mac?"

"Rifles. A hundred of 'em. Plan to sell the lot along the Pennsylvania border."

"I'll be your first customer."

"I know! It's another reason why I picked you up!" A snort from both men.

"Say, Mac. I'm not keen on Pennsylvania and west. Where're we headed?"

"To a little town called Gettysburg. Got family there. Nice and quiet."

@@@

Epilogue

The large dark gray stone has the look of an ancient time, pitted and weather worn, but with the sturdiness of permanency. At first glance it looks unfinished, as the stone begs to possess an obelisk on top of it. The monument is surrounded by a brick wall that could be easily scaled by a youngster, and a wrought iron gate allows the visitor to walk within its hallowed space.

Louis and Shannon walked slowly and separately among the dozens of headstones, many of which look original to the monument's placement. Pumpkin lay between two of them, either as a sentry or in repose.

Louis approached Shannon. "Hey!"

"Hey, *what?*"

"You have two different eye colors! You missing a contact or something?" Louis regretted the leap, and was ready to backpedal, not wanting to offend her.

Shannon's laugh was throaty and genuine. "No, *silly*, they're different. Green and blue. It unnerves people a little, and *there*, just like *you* now, guys get this stupid fish-mouth look." She continued to chuckle.

"Wow. I think it's really cool. It suits you!"

"My, you are a charmer. Well, my great-grandmother had them, and *her* grandfather had them. My nana practically *freaked* when she first saw them develop when I was a little girl. She was always sitting me on her lap and telling me tall tales of her great-grandfather in the Civil War, a *real* hero!

"Wow. That's even cooler. Is your grandfather buried here?" Louis tried to count and calculate the great-greats and gave up.

"Oh, no. He died at a ripe old age, in bed when he was *ninety*!" Her smile was warm and heartfelt, and she sighed audibly. "It's so peaceful here."

"Yes. Yes, it is." They spent many long minutes walking amongst the graves, silently reading each legible marker. The sun was high and reflected the leaves off the larger memorial, and the wind sounded like chimes, subtle and faint.

"Thank you for showing me this, Shannon. I've been here a few times, to the battlefield, but I haven't taken the time to learn anything new."

Shannon clapped twice softly. In a loud whisper, "Oh, I am *so happy* you're glad! This is better than just sitting and *waiting* for some kid to throw a ball near you, *right*?"

He had to chuckle. "Yeah, or to wait for some crazy chick to have her dog attack me!"

She bumped shoulders with him, and they both smiled looking in different directions. Louis walked over to where Pumpkin was laying down.

"Shannon. Look at these two headstones." He folded his arms in reflection.

"The same last name! Moas. Just initials, A and G. Same unit. Hmmm." She squinted.

He pointed to the stones, and asked, "Do you think they'll be remembered?"

"Oh, Louis. They are now. They *always* will be. They're here for everybody to see." She touched his hand. "Maybe they were father and son."

"They were brothers, I think."

As they walked out of the monument area, down a path to the main road to hike back to the Visitor Center,

Pumpkin started scratching and digging near a muddy hole, which appeared to erupt with rock and clay, surrounded by orange cones and yellow tape that was left by construction crews. Small pockets of repair were ubiquitous. Shovel work, no machinery. It did not detract from the peace.

"I like that they tend to all this, Shannon. Shows that they care."

"There is a lot of upkeep, yes. I love it here."

Louis wanted to say that he did, too, but did not want to spook this special girl. "Yeah, it's cool."

"*Pumpkin*! What are you *digging* at?" Louis liked how she punched her words.

He knelt and allowed the dog to smell the back of his hand, and it abruptly forgot what it had been pining for. Louis reached for a small object sticking out of the ground, incongruent in the dirt and rock and mud. He picked it up, stood, and showed it to Shannon.

"Look, it's a spoon, or something. An old metal one."

"Is it trash?"

"No, I don't think so."

"Let's show it to the ranger..."

The End

End Notes

The true historical movements of the 6th Regiment of Breckinridge's "Orphan Brigade" match the dates and times I have depicted in the book. I realized while I was developing **The March of the Orphans** that I would never be able to give an in depth account of the entire set piece battle. I have tried to write a respectful and historically accurate treatment of a fictitious unit of Rebel orphans within the true larger regiment and brigade. I chose small unit interactions and character development to speak of the people that made the history of this battle so unique. This is a novel with a historical basis in fact, and I do not pretend to be an expert.

My wife and I visited the **Stones River National Battlefield** outside of Murfreesboro, Tennessee, during a combined work and book signing trip to Nashville in November, 2013.

The grounds are beautiful, peaceful, and astonishing in well-preserved detail. The gravestones, thousands of them in remembrance of soldiers from all over our nation, circa 1863, are sobering.

What is equally impressive is the Visitor Center. The displays describe a battle where the field strength was over 41,000 Union soldiers and 35,000 CSA, and total casualties were almost 30% on both sides. These are staggering numbers, and while they make Stones River one of the bloodiest fights of the Civil War, except for regional devotees this fight is largely unknown. It is from the walk-through and reading of the displays that we discovered the catalyst for this novel: The Orphan Brigade.

The authority at the Stones River National Battlefield is Ranger Jim Lewis, who directed me to two chief research works that would provide the foundation I now craved to begin the project.

Blue & Gray Magazine, Volume XXVIII, Issue 6, contains Ranger Lewis' lengthy article "A Hard Earned Victory for Lincoln," which provided a concise history complete with no less than eighteen copyrighted maps depicting the field of battle and specific movement and placement of units. Ranger Lewis' article is wonderful and should be read first by anyone who seeks to know the hard facts, military tactics, and personalities that affected the battle. The rough map at the beginning of my novel is a tease.

Eyewitnesses at the Battle of Stones River, compiled and edited by David R. Logsdon, ©2002, 1989, is also a magnificent work. Mr. Logsdon put the actual letters and diary entries of both northern and southern soldiers in chronological order, and each page builds on the previous one. It is both fascinating and harrowing. Many of the writers of these letters did not survive the battle itself, let alone the war.

The magazine and book above are real works of love and history, and I am in Ranger Lewis' debt for the referral.

I hope **The March of the Orphans** inspires you to visit and take advantage of the wealth of history the Stones River National Battlefield possesses.

Travel safe.

@@@

Acknowledgements

The concept of a short series of books on unique and unheralded heroics of the Civil War was given to me after I published **The March of the 18th**. Gerald Tuttle, PhD, and USAF veteran, was an early enthusiast of my first novel, and continues to be my great friend, full of wonderful ideas. He has given me fascinating information, advice, and direction, and I am humbled and grateful.

Jim Lewis, Park Ranger at Stones River Battlefield National Park, also read a near complete work, and offered valuable advice. His encouragement and positive outlook are infectious, and his article referenced in the End Notes provides the outline for this book.

A lifetime of thank you's to Maureen and Matt, my wife and my brother, for reading the early draft and providing crucial feedback. Maureen softened the rough edges, and Matt characteristically attacked the manuscript with chisel and hammer. Special thanks to my friend Art D'Alessandro for his sage advice and key editing suggestions. It is a much better work because of their time and attention.

I have been blessed to have been able to give away several thousand dollars in royalties to wonderful veteran charities because of the support I have received for my writing endeavors. The plan remains unchanged, and I will continue to donate fifty percent of all royalties to selected charities for veterans. I pray this book can match the enthusiastic support received for **The March of the 18th**.

To all my readers and supporters, friends and fellow writers, you are all an inspiration.

Thank you.

@@@

Memento Lapsos Bellator
"Remember the Fallen Warrior"

CPSIA information can be obtained
at www.ICGtesting.com
Printed in the USA
LVOW04s1435220416
484879LV00024BB/348/P

9 781498 441858